The Adventures of Rockford T. Honeypot

Josh Gottsegen

Published by OneLight Publishing
Los Angeles, California
www.onelightpublishing.com

Library of Congress Control Number: 2019919212
ISBN Print: 978-0-9909270-5-1
ISBN Digital: 978-0-9909270-6-8

For Rose

CONTENTS

CONTENTS

Thank you to my wonderful parents and brother for your love and support. Carol and Peter for your guidance.
...And of course, my dog Olive.

"Be bold and blossom."

CHAPTER 1
GREEN-HUT MARKET 39

Deep in the forest, nestled between the trees, a dome-shaped warehouse of wood and glass seems to sprout from the soil. Inside, a multi-colored kaleidoscope of fresh fruits, vegetables, flowers, and nuts grows from end to end. Just outside, a menagerie of forest creatures, from lizards and chipmunks to monkeys and birds, mingle and shop at the trendy outdoor marketplace.

Perched high up on a branch, an elderly parrot startled by a howler monkey in transit, lets out an embarrassingly high-pitched squawk. A red feather drops from his wing and drifts toward the tables of carefully arranged fruit, where two hedgehogs sample pineapple on sale.

A gust of wind blows the feather toward the premiere check-out line, marked by a golden silk rope entwined with gold leaves and a dazzling golden carpet. A few well-to-do squirrels, apes, rabbits, and ring-tailed lemurs chat amongst themselves, complimenting one another on their designer jewels, eccentric hats, and lavish leaf-lined coats. The feather grazes the nose of a well-dressed gibbon. His super-sized sneeze throws him back into the mud, ruining his silk jacket and propelling the feather toward the regular checkout line.

The wait is abnormally long today, made even longer by a combination of the annual Purple Thursday Mega Sale and a missing orangutan salesclerk who called in sick. It doesn't take long for the waiting animals to lose patience, whip out their phones, and begin to complain on Whisker, Tropland's most popular social network.

The red feather glides toward an elegant, grey-haired chipmunk waiting in the growing line. As she catches the falling feather, her oversized red coat knocks over a basket of cherries from a table.

"Let me get those for you," a calm, chivalrous voice speaks from behind her.

She turns to see a handsome, well-dressed chipmunk picking up the spilled cherries. His ocean-blue eyes catch her attention.

"Thank you." She squints as she takes in his gracious smile. Something about him seems a little familiar. "Have we met before?"

"Oh, I suppose I have one of those cheeks," he replies, adjusting his plum-colored blazer.

Everything about this chipmunk exudes sophistication and class: from his snazzy suit, blue vest, and red bowtie, to his youthful light-brown fur and the distinguished gray stripe running from his forehead to his nose. Well, almost everything. On his nose sits a pair of circular eye-glasses with a purple vine holding the damaged left frame together.

A young chipmunk by his side snatches the final cherry, tossing it back on the table.

"Thank you. Is this your grandson?" the female chipmunk asks kindly.

"GREAT-grandson," the small boy pipes up as he plays with his green yo-yo.

"Of course, forgive me," she replies, taking a few seconds to break her gaze.

"Rockford T. Honeypot," he says, extending his paw. "This is my great-grandson, Theo."

"Heyooo!" belts out the boy, climbing up to his great-grandfather's shoulder, leaping off with a triple backflip.

"THE Rockford T. Honeypot?" she gasps, shaking his paw. "Shouldn't you be in the premiere checkout line? I've heard so many stories about you."

"Oh, dear. I'm just an ordinary chipmunk from Kona Valley." Rockford lets out a nervous chuckle and smooths his hair down awkwardly. He looks away, struggling to find something to comment on. "Say, I just love the scent of fresh jasmine flowers in full summer bloom, don't you?"

"Ordinary? There's nothing ordinary about you, from what I've heard," she persists, her eyes sparkling.

"And what did you hear? I'm as ordinary as lemon pie."

"Can we go now?" complains Theo, hopping onto the cherry table. "How much longer do we have to wait? I'm hungry! Do they have lemon pie?"

Rockford grabs him by the scruff of his neck and places him on the ground.

"Be patient, Theo. Paws on the sod, now. We talked about this."

"Can't you just say the ground? Cheeps, you're old-school, Great-granddad!"

"Age is a privilege, my pint-sized Honeypot," Rockford says, wiping off dirt from Theo's navy-blue shirt. "Oh, where are my manners? What is your name?"

"Who, me? Well, my name is Rosalina," she replies.

"A pleasure to meet you," smiles Rockford, wiping more moss from Theo's shoulder. "Theo, you look just like Chester, your grandfather, when he was your age. You know, this line hasn't moved, and we may be here for a short while. How about story time?"

"Story time? I'm not a pup. I'm eleven years old, if you knew anything about me," sasses Theo, rolling his big eyes.

"Is that really Rockford T. Honeypot?" whispers a woodpecker a few animals back.

"As in Honeypot, Inc.? He disappeared years ago," murmurs a squirrel to a young monkey with long, golden hair and a tail twice as long as he is tall.

"He's famous? Lemme get a closer look!" gushes the monkey as he bounces over numerous animals to get closer to Rockford.

"Not just famous; he's arguably the most successful and wealthiest animal in all of Tropland! I heard he even dated Cleopatra, the red fox heir to the Egyptian forest," says a weasel to the chipmunk waiting in line next to him.

"My cousin's friend's aunt's manicurist told us she used to see him at Hollygrove parties with the hottest Golden Age celebs!" mutters the chipmunk to a capybara, a beaver-like rodent five times his size.

"For reals?!" says the capybara. He tosses a few smaller chipmunks onto his back so they can have a better view. "I'm game for story time. Let's hear it!"

The animals shift out of their single-file line in order to form an audience closer to Rockford.

"I must admit, it's been a few moons since I've been back here," says Rockford, wiping debris off a broken tree stump with his handkerchief. "Theo, don't eat those nuts until we pay for them."

Theo spits four peanuts back into his basket. "Great-granddad. Nobody cares."

"Quit being a weasel! We wanna hear the story!" shouts a voice from somewhere back in the crowd.

"I resent that!" protests a weasel. "But I totally want to hear the story too."

The animals chatter amongst themselves, eagerly waiting to hear what the famous chipmunk has to say.

"You don't know much about me, do you?" Rockford whispers to Theo.

"Um… nope. We've only talked, like, three times," the boy grumbles back.

"I've been gone for a while and take full responsibility for my actions. However, considering what day it is, and why we're here, how about we make the best of it? Will you do that for me?"

"Fine. Tell your story." Theo sits near Rockford, fiddling with his yo-yo.

Rockford smiles slyly and stoops to give Theo a rock from the forest floor. "Think you can hit that purple sign on the green-hut wall?"

"The one that says thirty-nine? Obviously," booms Theo, who snatches the rock and, with all his might, tosses it directly at the center of the sign.

"Dunk! Nice one," Rockford approves, wiping his paws.

"You're so weird. It's your fault if I get in trouble!" snickers Theo.

"Did you know I built the very first Green-Hut Market with your great-grandmother? Our company, Honeypot, Inc., owns all the Green-Hut Markets in Tropland, including market forty-two for the bigger animals across the river."

"Really?" interrupts Rosalina.

"Really?" echoes Theo, cracking another peanut shell.

"There are a few things about my life that may surprise you, some of which I've never told anyone before."

"Yes! Origin story!" shouts the capybara. "All the best superheroes have origin stories."

"What else?" asks Theo.

"I learned to cook using fire with Tropland's finest chef. Flew across the great forest from coast to coast on wild hawks. Travelled to a hidden garden, where I learned ancient secrets from a species of chipmunk thought to have been extinct. Oh, and revolutionized Tropland's food and transport systems."

"Meh. Wanna see a new trick?" says Theo, throwing his yo-yo down and snapping it back with his other paw. The string gets caught on a branch and nearly breaks. "Dang! It's the lightning bolt. One of the hardest tricks."

"Lightning bolts can be tricky." Rockford adjusts his glasses. "I've seen many in just about every type of storm. From floods to fires, I've lost as much as I've loved. There's a good lesson to be learned about this yoo-yoo trick."

"Alright, tell the story, Great-granddad!" Theo exclaims, fixing his string. "And it's a yo-yo, not a yoo-yoo."

CHAPTER 2
GROWING UP HONEYPOT

My name is Rockford T. Honeypot. I grew up not too far from here, in the Kona Valley. My mother, Emma, was my best friend, and sweeter than a vine-ripened plum in season. Always wearing a flowing blue dress and smelling like fresh tea tree oil, her fur was more golden than the rays of the sun. She had a thin gray stripe, much like mine, right between her blue eyes. My mother's voice was as soft as a toucan's feather, unlike my father, Clarence. He was the roughest, toughest nutcracker across the forest, much like his father, Clarence, and his father, Clarence, and his father, Clarence, and… as you can imagine, a long lineage of Clarences. Over the years, twenty-two generations of Mr. Clarence Honeypot operated the flourishing family business, Clarence, Clarence, and Clarence; also known as CC&C.

CC&C was located mid-understory in the Kona Nut District. It was one of the largest distributors of raw walnuts and filbert nuts, also known as hazelnuts, in the forest. The business was thriving, but raising sixty-two children wasn't so economical. Most of my clothes were passed down from siblings who outgrew them. Even my eye-glasses, worn by Uncle Clarence for most of his life, became mine. Extra-large on my face, they served a dual purpose. Not only did they increase my vision, they protected my eyes from itchy pollen!

My short-tempered father was constantly barking and snarling at everyone in our family. With his dark eyes and pale gray fur, he looked perpetually angry. My father's arms were always folded, and his face could grow red as a tomato. The only time I ever saw him laugh was the time I got tangled in a spider web while helping my sister climb up a branch. The webbing tasted like unwashed cotton that made my mouth more dry than rotten almonds. She then shoved me off a fifth deck tree branch into a puddle of wet mud and bird droppings. They all had a good hoot and laughed for hours. Personally, I didn't get the joke. I had sixteen splinters and was exposed to that unsanitary swamp water! It took my mother the rest of the evening to scrub the dirt from my fur, buff my nails, and brush my tail until I reached an acceptable state of cleanliness.

Six weeks later, our tree-hut, built by my great-great-great-grandfather Clarence with his bare paws and claws, was demolished by termites. Back then, the ruthless termite mob would strike without warning. Not only did they eat unoccupied trees, but they would devour residential tree-huts to nothing more than dust! Even the Tropland police force, with its thriving campaign of stopping predatory attacks throughout the forest, didn't have an answer for the increase in organized termite crime.

Homeless, we had no choice but to pack our limited belongings and move ninety-four trees west and twelve branches down to a smaller tree-hut in a kapok tree. I was never fond of change, especially when the upper branches were inhabited by loud-mouthed ring-tailed lemurs, and my room was near blossoming flowers that emitted a stinky odor.

The new neighborhood was densely populated with a wide variety of chipmunk, squirrel, and marmot families. Most of the children my age were learning to count using scales on a pinecone. I was using the same pinecones to understand spiral geometry and solve complex mathematical formulas. For me, learning was my superpower, as was exceptional hygiene skills. To them, I was different. I was the weird 'furpee boy' with no friends. Kids stayed away from me because of a childish rumor. Apparently, I had the highly contagious 'furpee disease' that made your skin itch worse than forest mites.

Being alone never bothered me; a reader is never alone. When I wasn't whiskers deep in a new book, I was writing in my journal, or playing rock, paper, scissors with my imaginary sidekick, Norby. I was plenty satisfied without the distraction of my twenty-five sisters, or thirty-six pea-brained brothers, all named Clarence. Over time, Clarences one through thirty-six had become friends with the neighborhood bully, Braxton McFudden, a chipmunk my age whose family owned over a dozen trees in our neighborhood grove. Somehow, Braxton's superpower was never getting in trouble nor blamed for his devious pranks.

"Furpee boy!" Braxton yelled.

My brothers circled around me, chanting his name like they were part of an ancient, uncivilized pack. Whether on a branch or out in the open field, this happened at least twice a month.

"Who's ready for a furpee cleanse?" he yelled again as I tried to escape past the locked arms of all the Clarences keeping me captive.

With Braxton's arms wrapped around my head, I felt the

pain from his claws scratching against the back of my neck.

"This is horseradish, Braxton! Stop it!" I screamed.

"Weakford T. Honeypot!" shouted my brothers in unison.

"I'm doing you a favor," sneered Braxton in a voice dripping with condescension. "I'll scratch the furpee clean off your head!"

"Stop it, Braxton! I mean it!" I cried in pain.

"Keep going, Braxton! He ain't no Clarence," hollered one of my brothers.

"Say it and I'll stop!" Braxton badgered.

"I'm a furpee chipmunk, short and stump, I love to eat worms, and I'm a chump," I cried with embarrassment and pain.

I was bullied relentlessly in my youth. Sometimes I was so upset, I would cry in my mother's arms. She calmed me down, and when I was ready, we did our 'minute limit.'

"Close your eyes, Captain Rockford T," she said softly, gently massaging my head. "Close your eyes, count to sixty. This is the last time we allow ourselves to feel these negative thoughts and emotions."

After sixty seconds, we would take a deep breath, and just like the sun burns the clouds away, let it all go without giving it one more thought. This was our secret that made us feel better.

-Back to Green-Hut Market 39-

"I once got my head stuck in an orange tree!" a young, long-tailed monkey interrupts. "True story!"

"Nobody cares!" yells Theo.

"Rude!" belts the monkey as he jumps up high, wraps his tail around a branch, and swings toward them. Theo's mouth falls open in laughter as the monkey flips onto his head.

"There's no need to quibble," says Rockford. "What's your name?"

"Randy Randerson. Call me Randy," the monkey says from upside-down.

"Randy. Theo. My mother and I used to read stories about the heroic Captain James T. He famously wrote, 'Learn to deal with the bees if you want to enjoy the honey.' What does that mean to you?"

"Why deal with bees when the honey is on sale?" says Theo, pointing to a table of assorted honey.

"Agreed," Randy replies as he flips back onto his feet.

"So much to learn, young Honeypot," Rockford says with a chuckle. "Let's continue."

--

I'd spend most of my days learning about the forest, animals, math, and science with my mother. She used to bring home books every week from the local university's library. I read them all, from encyclopedias and law reviews to fictional classics such as 'The Myth of the Pear Princess' and 'Homer's Marsh.' Now and then, she'd come home with a treat, another book from my favorite series: 'The Adventures of Captain James T. Rockford.'

Nothing gave me more goosebumps than reading a new Captain James T. adventure. His voyages through the forest canopy to explore strange new kingdoms, seek out new species, and discover unusual cultures and cuisines across the never-ending jungle kept me awake all night, dreaming about my future! I idolized Captain James T. Aside from being frightened of large animals in the canopy and petrified of the bugs, bacteria, and germs living throughout the jungle, we were cut from the same vine.

"Mother, how did Captain James T. afford such lavish travel adventures?" I asked her one evening, bouncing around the room in my purple captain's cape.

"You see those shining bright lights twinkling above the tree-tops?" she asked, looking fondly out the window. "Those are unshelled diamonds. Captain James T. would climb up the tallest mountain and grab one when he needed a boost. In the right paws, they can change the entire forest with their glow."

It was that evening when I knew my fate was sealed beyond the stinky flowers of the kapok tree. One day, I was gonna grow as tall as a banana and set sail as Captain Rockford T. Honeypot on an adventure to the unshelled diamonds!

Year after year, my brothers and Braxton would continue to wreak havoc. Playing keep-away with my books, burying them deep in the forest floor, or "accidentally" bumping me off the tree branches, they were a thorn in my side.

That is, until I sprouted like a coconut!

I may have been scared of climbing the beetle-infested trees of the forest, but I was suddenly gifted with lightning quick legs to scamper across the forest floor!

"You'd better run, Weakford. Run!" shouted my brothers in the distance as I ran faster than a flash flood in summer. My cape waved in the wind as I kept running through parts of the forest not meant for a small chipmunk. Dodging beetles, falling acorns, and slugs throughout the duff, I ran until I reached the open strawberry fields of Easelwood. I'd sanitize a small area with lavender-scented paw soap and relax, daydreaming of adventures to find the unshelled diamonds.

Let's fast-forward a couple more years, after the brown and white stripes down my back had darkened. When I was thirteen, I took over CC&C. As my mother proclaimed, my father decided to retire and live a 'stress-free lifestyle.' The collective intelligence of the entire Clarence brothers was akin to a rafter of wild turkeys, so taking over the family business fell on my lap like a falling hazelnut.

I remember that dreadful morning like it was just yesterday. It was freezing, and my lips were quivering.

SPLAT!

A wet, cold leaf dropped onto my face. I looked up to find my father standing over me, picking food from his teeth.

"Son. You and me never done seen eye to eye, okay? Not jus' 'cause you're the runt of this scurry," he mumbled.

I tried to stand up, but he stuck his paw in my face. I was horrified! Not only did it smell like burnt cedar wood, but it was cold and flu season and I was certain he hadn't washed his paws.

"I ain't finished, Rockford. Okay? Your mama tells me you've got big dreams to change the forest. You can dream all night while you sleep, but when yer awake, you do what I say. These cheeks have seen enough walnuts and filberts for twelve lifetimes, so I'm leaving you in charge of the business while I'm gone. Some of yer sisters an' hopefully yer brothers are gettin' married soon to live on their own an' have babies. Mama and I are goin' to stay with yer Uncle Clarence for a few months, so yer brothers will run the nut hunts and crackin'. You'll pay them right. Okay?

"I'll pay them appropriately based on merit," I explained.

"Now you watch that mouth of yers. The nuts on shrubs are prime for pickin' this summer, but money don't grow on these trees. Filberts do! I ain't askin'. I'm tellin'. Okay?

If he says 'okay' one more time, I thought.

"Don't let yer brothers charge you too much now, okay?" He barked once again. "Now get up! Yer late for work!"

Two days later, my parents' bags were packed, and a private transport goose flew in, right on time, to pick them up.

My mother picked up a stone from the ground and held it in the shade. "Tell me, what color is this stone?"

"Black."

Then, she held the stone high above my head. The sunlight revealed a beautiful purple stone casting a glow on my white button-down shirt.

"Oh, it's a purple amethyst! I read about them in geology books."

"Beauty is everywhere," she said, pinching my cheeks. "Sometimes you just need to look from a different angle. Live long and blossom, Captain Rockford T."

After they left, I started to get a grip on the business. I had plans to increase sales with revolutionary ideas but was bullied into paying my brothers triple the normal rate for cracking the nuts during the cold winter.

Over the course of several months, Clarences one through twenty-six took advantage of me while I bankrupted the company. What took several hundred years of Honeypots to build, I had destroyed in just six months.

We were officially broke.

Arriving back from his vacation, my father was so furious, he shoveled walnuts into his mouth until he nearly toppled over.

"What you got to say for yerself?" he barked. "Yer as useless as a three-toed sloth!"

"First of all, it wasn't my fault!" I protested. "Second of all, while notoriously slow, the three-toed sloths are agile swimmers compared to their nocturnal ancestors, the two-toed sloths. So, claiming they are useless is based on nothing short of discrimination!"

"You learn that hare-brained language from yer mother? I swear I don't know what yer saying half the time. Okay? Okay! All I know is yer a failure, and I'm ruined. We're all ruined! This was my fault. I should have chosen a Clarence to run the company! What in the gingersnaps was I thinking? That's it. THAT'S IT! Pack your bags, Honeypots. We're moving. AGAIN! This time to Rica Canyon! You can all thank yer brother for ruining everything!" my father yelled.

"Horseradish! It wasn't my fault," I pleaded.

I took the amethyst stone, which I still carried in my pocket, and threw it at my father. My aim was off, and I hit one of my brothers in the head.

"Clarence! Let's talk about this privately," my mother pleaded.

"No. No! I've made my decision." His face changed from a light tan to a tomato red as he held my brother back from chasing me. "WE'RE MOVING! Start packing right now. Everyone! Except you." He pointed one shaking finger at me. "No, no, no. Not you, boy. Best your name isn't Clarence after all. You failed us, and there ain't no more room for failure in this family! What was I thinking?!"

That week, the Honeypots moved east to live with my Uncle Clarence. Well, the whole family except for yours truly. It took an entire flock of six private transport geese to fly them away. My mother was the last to board, with my father yelling "Hurry yer furry tail!"

"Keep your cheeks full and always move forward," she said with a tear in her eye. She kissed my forehead, then handed me a folded-up piece of paper.

"What's this?" I sniffled.

"I believe in you," she whispered, kissing my forehead once again. "I love you so much. Don't you ever give up."

And just like that, they were gone. The geese flew away above the canopy trees, leaving nothing behind but memories and tears.

"Hey, Furpee!" yelled Braxton from across the branch. "Why don't you go inside, now that your dull-witted family abandoned you? I heard there's a python in these woods hungry for Honeypot!"

Loud-mouthed Braxton's insults didn't affect me. I opened the note, but could barely read my mother's writing, my eyes filling with tears. Uncle Clarence's address in Rica Canyon, written in her unmistakable writing, was all I had.

I could understand her needing to leave to make sure the rest of the family was taken care of, but now who was going to take care of me? I thought to myself, heavy-hearted.

I ran to my bed and cried for hours, only to find solace in reading 'The Adventures of Captain James T.' Later that evening, I had a profound realization. It was time for me to make a choice: move forward with a life of mystery and adventure, or follow the transport geese to Rica Canyon and beg my father for forgiveness.

I knew my mother thought I was going to follow shortly after they left, but I wasn't going back with my tail tucked between my legs. Destiny was climbing up the branch, tugging on my arm, and calling me in the opposite direction. Two days later, armed with my journal, four peas, half a tomato, a backpack filled with hazelnuts, my purple amethyst stone, my purple cape, and just enough of my mother's lavender-scented 'Red's Paw Soap,' I was ready. I couldn't afford to buy a feather on a string for two shells, but I was going to live a life full of adventure!

CHAPTER 3
MORNING OF EVE

After several days of wandering around the forest, I felt a bit parched. It was the start of winter, much frostier than anticipated. Despite the chilly temperatures, I always found time to stop and smell the roses. That is, until the floral scent of jasmines carried me a few trees further. Next, the aromatic fragrance of blossoming sweet peas and lilacs sang to my nostrils. Stopping at every flower patch on my path in order to get a whiff of good sniffs, I heard snoring from inside the closed petals of a lovely, red-flecked, pumpkin-colored tulip.

"Go away, Mum. It's a holiday an' I don't have school," chirped a high-pitched voice with an accent I'd never heard before.

"It's biologically impossible for a flower to speak. Hello? Is anyone inside the flower?" I asked.

A small white harvest mouse poked his head through the petals, rubbing his sleepy eyes.

"Was I asleep? Pollen does that to us." The mouse wrinkled

his face up in concentration. "Wait a tick, do I know you?"

"No, sir."

"Sir? Come now, lad, call me Joel." The mouse crawled out of the flower, stretching his body. "Oooh, it's a bit nippy out, isn't it? Hey, boys! Let's take five underground, shall we?"

Four more mice crawled out from closed tulips. They all wore the same black blazers, grey hoodies and matching pants.

"How long were we out?" one asked.

"Didn't even know I was asleep," another replied.

"Who's this lad?" a third interjected.

Joel leaned on my paw to stretch his back legs. "This fine lad was our wake-up call. Join us underground for a bite?"

They showed me how to dig proper holes in the subfloor for both safety and warmth. It was an act of survival on one paw, a heap of dirt, bacteria, insects, and worms on the other. I typically stayed away from the forest subfloor for sanitary reasons even though my body kept shivering from the cold.

Fun Fact: It turns out that mice eat fifteen to twenty meals a day! We dug ourselves a warm, comfy burrow underground, where I stuffed my cheeks with more oranges, plums, berries, and peanuts than I'd ever had in my entire life!

We stayed together for two weeks, filling our bellies until the sun melted the chilly frost from the forest. It was fun while it lasted, my first sleepover with friends! Turns out these mice were in a band together called The Mischiefs. As much as I wanted to join them as a rock star chipmunk, my tummy was twisted from too many berries.

I kept a bland diet for the next month: hazelnuts for breakfast, brunch, lunch, dinner, and an occasional late-night treat. By the time I ate half the bag, my cheeks were as rough as a groundhog's tail. For a relatively small chipmunk, I have mighty jaw strength, enough to crack hazelnuts all day. Likely a trait I inherited from my father and his big mouth.

One dark and cold evening, the bugs were buzzing so loud I could barely hear my own thoughts. Coming upon the shore of a freshwater lake, and being super thirsty, I thought I had found Treasure Island! I looked around to ensure no dangerous animals were nearby. Then, like a pole-vaulting beaver, I jumped up as high as I could in the upside-flamingo position and dove face-first.

DONK!

The notion of a frozen lake must have skipped my mind. My whiskers felt the chill of the ice a split second before I knocked myself out cold!

By the time I regained consciousness, I could hear the sound of crackling firewood and smell fresh acorns. The realization that I was in a nice, cozy bed five sizes bigger than my own took me by surprise.

My head was throbbing with a big welt.

I blinked several times to make sure this wasn't a dream. Wall to wall ultra-luxurious, warm sapele wood floors? A covered patio encased in mesh screening to keep all the insects out? No dust? No bugs? No germs? *I must be dreaming!*

I leaned my face against the mesh screen, peeking over the edge at the magnificent view of the lush Kona Valley. This had to be two hundred branches up in a giant sequoia tree! I was looking down at flying hawks while the lemurs swinging across the vines looked like dancing hamsters.

"Well, look who woke up bright-eyed and bushy-tailed, ya nutty nut!" shouted a voice from behind me.

A bag of ice soared toward my face. I ducked, and it hit the wall. Ice cubes shot across the entire room.

"Sorry. Aside from catching a seasonal cold, I'm not much of an athlete," I said, timid of the muskrat twice my size.

"I'm a chef, not your nurse. That mess is yours to clean up," grumbled the muskrat. "You were gonna freeze your cute, fluffy tail off out there! Lucky I was out searching for basil."

"Thank you for the hospitality, madam," I said, rubbing my stiff neck.

It felt naked—something was missing!

My cape was gone! "Did you see my cape? It's purple. A purple cape?!"

"Calm down. Nope, no cape." She held my bag in the air. "No chance a scrawny, non-athletic chipmunk like yourself could harvest these beauties. How many hazelnuts you got in here, anyway?"

I sighed, feeling defeated.

A captain without a cape? I'm doomed.

"Forty-six. Would you like one?" I offered.

"Oh, happy Tuesday. At least your noggin still works. You can stay until your head's right, but it'll cost ya two hazelnuts per day. Deal?"

"Yes. Thank you, madam."

"Stop calling me madam! I'm Eve Pippens. Nice to officially meet ya. If you're feeling better, wanna go for a jog across the canopy branches later? The sunset is beautiful here."

"I'm Rockford T. Honeypot," I said, holding my amethyst stone close to my heart. "I love to jog, but I'd like to rest a bit more, if you don't mind?"

"Make yourself at home, Rockford!"

As it turned out, Eve was renting a luxury tree-hut for a few months while learning about the local cooking styles. She was known for her restaurant, The Evening Musk, in Brentwood, South Tropland—a four-hour flight on a transport goose, or a two-month hike from here.

A premiere chef, Eve had both commercial and personal

fire licenses. Mind you, at this point in my life, I had never seen a controlled fire. Tropland Federal Law 2212 prohibits the use of fire without a government-issued fire safety license. That first night, she cooked her signature tomato basil soup with fresh herbs. The juicy, plump tomatoes, fresh garlic, onions, and aromatic smell of fresh basil had me salivating like a jungle puppy. Though I was timid around the burning fire, the creamy and flavorful soup was so good, it made my ears tingle with every spoonful. I had grown up eating raw fruits, veggies, and nuts, so I'd never had anything like this before.

Most of my time was spent in the kitchen cleaning up and learning what Eve called 'Modernist Cuisine.' It was a fancy way of cooking with a touch of this, a dash of that, and a final pinch to tickle the tasty buds.

Back home, my mother only knew how to cook family style. This was cooking for just one or two mouths at a time. It seemed wacky at first, but this way of cooking became my new passion. I went from eating raw hazelnuts to mixing them with fresh greens, adding a touch of pear, a dash of citrus zest, a pinch of salt, and behold... a hazelnut pear salad!

On day twenty-three of our friendship, as I was cleaning up after dinner, Eve came bursting into the kitchen.

"Say, Rockford. You want to head back to Brentwood with me? I could use an extra paw cleaning up the restaurant, and Farley sure could use the help. Plus, we've got mounds of hazelnuts in Brentwood, I'll replenish your backpack tenfold. What do you say?"

"Is a one-legged chipmunk busy in a sandbox?" I jumped up with excitement, knocking the table and sending plates and utensils clattering to the ground. I knelt down to pick them up. "Oh, dear. Sorry. Yes, I'd love to go!"

"Come on, ya nutty nut," she replied. "Staying in one place

for too long makes you comfortable. Comfort makes you lazy, and lazy makes you boring! Are you boring, little Rockford T. Honeypot?"

"No… I'm cautious," I tried to explain.

"Don't be such a house mouse. Want to go for a jog? I'll tell you all about Brentwood?"

"And risk a cramp after we just ate? I appreciate the gesture, but no thank you," I replied.

She shrugged. "Alright. We leave at dawn. Be bold, Rockford. Goodnight."

Be bold? I wondered.

Even without his cape, Captain James T. would rise to the challenge and explore Brentwood. My life was unfolding like the pages of a great adventure book. It was time to branch out, be bold, and explore!

But first, I needed to stock up on more Red's Paw Soap just to be safe. One could only imagine the germs and bacteria waiting for me in Brentwood.

CHAPTER 4
THE EVENING MUSK

Eve bought us one-way tickets on a premiere transport goose from Kona Valley to Brentwood. She purchased all four seats to carry the extra food, spices, and nuts she'd bought over the last month. It was my first time flying high above the rainforest treetops. We rode inside a private, comfy carriage fastened on the goose with a protective roof and doors on each side.

The doors had blinds we could open to see the forest from this new perspective. The tops of the tree crowns looked like groves of broccoli populated with birds, monkeys, and other primates going about their morning. The four-hour flight felt like a few short minutes as I was mesmerized by the enchanting waterfalls, canyons, and never-ending green trees. At this height, I could even see the power vines, built by beavers using the river force that provided Tropland with safe electricity.

I held my purple amethyst stone toward the bright sunlight and felt a chill of excitement. I was living the life of Captain James T. on a real adventure!

As we descended, the forest was sparkling with life. Pink and green flowers, thick leaves, and rubbery trees were connected by bridges, vines, and walkways through the canopy connecting its lively community.

"South Tropland has a higher volume of rain than Kona Valley. Hope you brought your raincoat," Eve said, eating a sweet-smelling tangerine.

"Do I smell yellow star flowers in blossom?" I asked, sticking my nose out the window. "I'm so excited! The southernmost point of South Tropland is covered in water, inhabited animals I've only read about in stories. I wonder if I should trim my nails to stay clean in this muddy forest floor."

"Forest floor? We call it the duff in these woods," said Eve.

'Yes, I know it's called the duff. Did you know a pawful contains enough bacteria and parasites to keep you on the log for weeks?"

"A chipmunk who trims his nails? You sure are nutty!"

The Evening Musk was a charming bamboo restaurant built on a broken pine tree that had snapped in half during a thunderstorm many moons ago. The tree stump configuration allowed Eve to build a custom kitchen within the hollow bark near the first line of branches and construct the restaurant's dining area on the second floor above. There, an inviting smell of fresh herbs and two dozen red wooden tables, each big enough to fit a scurry of twenty squirrels, were attractively arranged.

We had a couple of restaurants back home, but my mother used to say, "They have toxins in their food," so we stayed away.

"FIRE!" I yelled as soon as I entered the kitchen of The Evening Musk.

Two large flames were raging from the floor. I involuntarily

exact same caterpillar-shaped birth mark on their left cheek. The twins even moved in the exact same manner! The Brentwood Brothers worked hard, saving to open a soup kitchen in their hometown. They offered to rent me a bedroom in their tree-hut.

-Back to Green-Hut Market 39-

"Let's get to some action, Captain Rockford!" shouts Randy as he hops up on his tail.

"I'm with the monkey, Great-granddad. If you're telling the story, don't make it a history lesson."

"Alright. Less babble, more dabble. Got it," Rockford says, cleaning his eyeglasses. "I suppose I could share the time I got stuck in the fire pipes? Or when I got lost for a week searching for the library?"

"Ladies and gentlefolks, we are officially livestreaming from Green-Hut Market 39!" shouts Holly, a woodpecker hanging from a tree branch. Wearing a coral pink and purple dress to contrast with her bright red hair, she's filming herself with her new phone. "Follow me on Whisker, HollyBubbles3. Don't forget to share, like, heart, and comment! Hashtag 'Rockford.' Hashtag 'Epic Story.'"

"Hashtag 'Origin Story!'" a voice yells from the crowd.

"Oh dear," says Rockford, blushing as he accidently bumps into Rosalina. For a brief moment, they lock eyes. "How do I look?"

"You look like you've been wanting to tell this story for quite some time, Mr. Honeypot."

Rockford fixes his bowtie. "For the record, I did return my books to that library. I may have been late, but I'm no outlaw.

CHAPTER 5

THE MIRACLE AT EVENING MUSK

DINK!

DINK!

"Missed two in a row! One more try, or it's kitchen duty for Rhubarb!" hollered Farley with the loudest, raspiest laugh.

Every night, we played a game of Dunk in the kitchen, where we took turns as the 'Skipper.' The Skipper made two decisions for the game: first, to choose the zone where we tried to toss unshelled hazelnuts into a soup pot. Sometimes the zone was behind the vegetable peel counter, from the peanut barrel, or even upside down on the spice shelves. We each had three hazelnuts; whomever tossed the least number of hazelnuts in the pot lost.

The Skipper's second decision was much more fun: deciding the evening chores for the loser. It was usually scrubbing the restaurant floors or picking up produce in the early morning.

Dink was the sound when the nut missed and bounced off

the pot.

Dunk was the sound when the nut landed inside.

It was a fun game, but unlike rock, paper, scissors with Norby, I could never win!

I picked the zone that evening: second step, standing on one leg. Everyone made at least one shot, and I had missed two in a row. The loser had to stay late and scrub both the kitchen and restaurant floors.

Balancing on one leg, my eyes fixated on the black soup pot. I was so focused, all the forest sounds softened to the point where I could only hear one thought: *Please don't miss.*

DINK!

Simon and Leo laughed so hard they fell to the floor.

"Rhubarb is out!" shouted Farley as he laughed his deep, uncontrollable laugh. "He throws like a butterfly!"

"Ah, horseradish!" I yelled, kicking over a bucket of chopped acorns.

"Rockford loses again! How many nights in a row has it been?" asked Eve while the rest of the crew got ready to leave for the night.

"One hundred and thirteen."

"Don't stay up too late. You need your beauty sleep," she teased, walking out of the kitchen. "Goodnight, dink master!"

We'd had a family of ten hamsters dine for dinner earlier that evening, food was all over the restaurant, under tables, in corners, even up on the ceiling. They were pocket-sized pigs, if you asked me, it took me a few hours to clean up.

Irritated, agitated, and hungry, I stayed at the restaurant all evening. I created all sorts of my own dishes, from fluffy brown rice with olive oil to broccolini shavings in tomato sauce. After an hour of binge eating, my tummy was sticking out like a pot-bellied hamster.

My first official cooking frenzy left the kitchen a disaster. Too full to clean up, I practiced my dunk shots from various zones. Throwing miss after miss, I got so irritated, I grabbed a pan and broke a hazelnut shell. After removing the nut from the shell fragments, then taking a small nibble for good luck, I tossed it toward the soup pot.

DUNK!

Sweet butternut bliss!

I made five more in a row!

A loud knock at the front door caught me off guard.

Who would be here so late?

The knocking became pounding. I hoofed it upstairs.

"Yes?" I inquired through the wooden door.

"Hi. My name's Danny. I live five trees southeast of here. The winds are blowing strong toward our tree-hut this evening. Would you mind putting out your fire?"

I opened the door to a white rabbit in a blue robe.

"Much obliged," he continued. "Our newborn baby is trying to fall asleep, and I'm afraid the smoke is giving him a runny nose. Hey now, this place smells rather crisp! Happen to have fresh mint? My wife and I love mint tea."

I gave the friendly rabbit a handful of fresh mint as an apology for keeping them up late. For a rabbit claiming to be tired, he sure was hopped up. Danny went on for a few minutes, chatting about how proud he was of his beautiful new son.

I wished the rabbit a pleasant evening and closed the door behind him. Danny was a friendly guy, but he stirred up gloom deep in my belly. Maybe it was the indigestion, but it made me think about my father. He never felt admiration for me as Danny had for his son. The truth is, I don't think my father ever liked me.

I looked out the window at the unshelled diamonds in the sky, a tear ran down my cheek.

"Mother, I'm sorry," I whispered. "I'm doing my best to be bold and blossom, but it's hard. I know you can't hear me, so I might as well be talking to the leaves. You always said changing the forest was my destiny. How is that possible? I can barely toss a hazelnut into a soup pot."

For several minutes, I couldn't take my eyes off the unshelled diamonds twinkling high above the tree-tops. They were talking to me, but I couldn't hear from so far away.

Suddenly, a strong, nutty smell tickled the tips of my whiskers.

I followed the mouth-watering trail through the whole restaurant. With each sniff, I detected a slightly new intriguing aroma.

Pea-like?

Creamy?

Chocolaty?

I followed the trail down toward the kitchen.

What in the leapin' lizards is that smell?

My body was gliding through the air, following the nutty, delicious scent. When I got to the kitchen, I realized the fire was still on and the pot was heating up off to the side.

"Nuts!"

I darted over and used two sticks to remove the hazelnuts from the pot and place them on a dry towel. There had been olive oil left over in the pot from my rice, and by some means it had transformed the nuts. They were soft and simply beautiful! The husks, or skin, around the nut looked loose, so I used a towel to gently remove them.

In all my years surrounded by hazelnuts, I'd never seen them look quite like this. It was unique, transformed. Darker, yet more tender. I'll never forget taking that first bite. As Eve would say, 'it had an entirely different flavor profile.' It was rich, buttery, smooth, and left an aftertaste that made me crave another!

-Back to Green-Hut Market 39-

"Wait a honeydew moment. You mean to tell me you were the VERY FIRST to roast a nut in all of Tropland?" asks Randy, hopping up on his tail.

"That's what he said, monkey brains!" bursts Theo, spinning his yo-yo close to Randy's face.

"Get this goofy thing away from me." Randy strikes the yo-yo to the ground with his long tail.

Just as the boys start wrestling, Rockford grabs Theo by the scruff of his neck and holds him up high, pumping his fists in the air like he's won a fight.

"He started it!" shouts Theo.

Rockford places Theo next to Randy.

"The two of you shake, or story time is over."

"Shake, kid!" yells a voice from the distance.

"*Story time?* Great-granddad, we discussed this," Theo says, rolling his eyes again.

Holly flies in closer with her phone, filming Theo and Randy.

A chant comes from a few animals: "Shake, shake, shake, shake!"

The boys take notice of their new fame and shake paws.

"And for my next trick, the famous lightning bolt," says Theo, spinning his yo-yo and retracting it back successfully with his other paw. "Woo!"

"Nice trick, Theo," says Rockford. "We succeed because

we learn from our mistakes. Shall we continue?"

"Fine." Theo shrugs, noticing Holly's camera is no longer focused on him.

CHAPTER 6
TASTING SUCCESS

Eve, Farley, Leo, and Simon arrived at the restaurant the next morning while I was fast asleep on the kitchen floor. During the evening, I had created a masterpiece of a mess in the kitchen; herbs, nut shells, salt, and husks were scattered from floor to ceiling.

"Rockford, ya nutty nut!" yelled Eve. "Someone thought to have a party last night here in my kitchen? What in the mango tango happened here?"

"Don't eat those in the corner. I burnt a few throughout the night. But try these!" I passed her a basket of cooked hazelnuts mixed with fresh herbs.

"Rhubarb, you dopey chip!" said Farley. "What gives you the right to cook in a kitchen that ain't yers? And you started a fire without a license?"

He sniffed the bowl of nuts, then ate one, transforming from an angry, bitter fella to a soft, happy, lovable one in moments. "Good nectar of Newton! How'd you cook these?"

Simon and Leo each ate a hazelnut. So overwhelmed with emotion, tears of bliss ran down their cheeks. They gave each other a heartfelt hug.

"Cheers!" chirped Simon.

"To both ears!" repeated Leo.

"Eve. Try Rhubarb's nuts! Rhubarb, how'd you do cook these?" Farley tossed one to Eve, who caught it, sniffed it, then nibbled on it.

Everyone waited for her reaction. She still looked upset that her kitchen was a mess, but I saw her tail secretly wag.

"A toast to Chef Rockford!" Simon and Leo shouted joyfully. "Cheers to both ears!"

Farley filled his cheeks with more nuts. "A… roast! Rhubarb, reese ruts are dericious!"

"A toast, not a roast!" Simon laughed hysterically. "But a roast to Rockford works, too!"

"Rockford," said Eve with an authoritative tone, "first, you're going to clean up my kitchen better than you've ever cleaned anything before. Then, you're going to explain how you made these. They… are delicious! Crisp, nutty, and boosted with a rich flavor profile!"

With that, she grabbed the whole basket of nuts and ran out of the kitchen, tail still wagging.

"Well done!" Simon smacked me on the back with a grin. "The boss approves. A 'roast' to our good pal and new chef, Rockford!"

The next few months were a whirlwind of excitement. The group insisted we call our new method of cooking 'roasting.' We perfected some recipes with a few extra pinches, drizzles, and touches, while creating a brilliant three-part roasting plan.

First, Farley built a new oven specifically for roasting. We called it 'the pit,' built with dark brown mud and rocks. It was round, with an enclosed space for a fire.

Second, we had to figure out how to set the oven to the right temperature. This was tricky, as the nuts could go from toasty to burnt faster than a frog leap. Since we already used a dash of olive oil to prevent the nuts from sticking, Eve came up with the brilliant idea of placing popcorn kernels in the oven. When seven kernels popped, we knew the temperature was just right.

Third and most importantly, we made a promise to each other to keep this method a secret.

"No matter the conditions or the weather," rallied Eve, "we tell nobody. Every big and bite-sized taste bud is gonna crave these beauties. This is gonna change the forest."

"To cookin'!" said Farley.

"To good foods!" chirped Simon.

"To good moods!" yelped Leo.

Eve gave me a big hug. "To our Nutty Nut!"

"To family!" I replied joyfully.

Modernist Cuisine Digest: Magazine Publication #43b
Snippet from article, "The Roasted Revolution is here to stay!"
Written by Rhondy H.B. Buttersworth

Actions speak louder than words in Tropland Rainforest as The Roasted Revolution has arrived. A delectable treat created by Master Chef Eve Pippens has taken the rainforest by a thunderous belly storm. Some wait in line for hours to buy roasted nuts in bulk. Many wait just as long, if not longer, for a seat in her restaurant, The Evening Musk, to enjoy a fresh batch. I myself have had the pleasure of trying the roasted hazelnut with cinnamon. The creamy flavor is worth the wait. Not since the discovery of brown rice and oatmeal has a movement so shaped our bellies! Every chef in the forest is trying to figure out the secret, but nobody has yet figured out the magic. Master Chef Eve is riding the winds to the top of the forest. If you're reading this now, you absolutely, positively must come and taste this tasty treat!

Eve had become the most popular chef in all of Tropland. Interviews, appearances, and attending fine gala events throughout the forest were just a pawful of the activities she performed on a weekly basis.

With the line to get into the restaurant growing faster than bamboo, the stress of keeping up the kitchen began to turn Farley's hair gray. While Eve reaped the forest-wide benefits of our roasting success, we worked from sunrise to twilight, struggling without her. We only saw her five times that year! Without Eve to lead our group in the midst of all the triumph and chaos, we were falling apart.

"While Eve is out prancing her tail, actin' Queen of the Jungle, I'm stuck workin' overtime, cookin' these nuts and not gettin' any respect!" yelled Farley across the kitchen. "Rhubarb, we're too talented to do the busy work of other folks."

He threw most of the hazelnuts and popcorn kernels in his large orange backpack.

"But if we work as a team, we can accomplish anything!" I said in an attempt to motivate him.

"Don't be so naïve. I'm gonna start my own restaurant with my own style. My own dishes. My own kitchen! I'll call it 'Farley's Feast!' Do me a kindness, when you see Eve, tell her…just tell her I'm sorry… and good luck. Do what ya love, Rhubarb."

He gave me a strong hug. In spite of his repulsive body odor, it was a warm embrace.

"What am I supposed to do now?" I asked.

"Yer a grown chipper. Figure it out."

He took off his chef apron and threw it over my head. At the time, I felt a gust of sadness as Farley called it quits. Not just because his apron hadn't been washed for weeks, but because he was the webbing that kept this kitchen together.

Another few weeks passed before Eve finally came home to find her restaurant closed for business. She was as angry as a poison arrow frog on Valentine's Day. I tried to take over for Farley, but couldn't keep up with such high demand. It reminded me once again that leaving a business in my paws was a terrible decision. Now, for the second time, I planted a business in the dirt, failing miserably.

I held my amethyst stone throughout every zone in the kitchen.

Beauty is everywhere, I reminded myself. *Soooo, why can't I find it?*

That evening, we had a group meeting. Simon and Leo decided it was time to return home to fulfill their dream of running a soup kitchen.

"Until we meet again, my friends," said Simon.

"My friends, until we meet again," repeated Leo.

Eve was planning a roasting tour later that month, so she decided to keep the restaurant closed until she returned.

"Rockford, this ain't your fault. I hope you don't take it personal," she said.

"Take what personal?"

"In all my interviews and magazines, I said I was the one who discovered roasting. Every paw, web, and foot is trying to duplicate our recipe. Not a chef comes within two shakes of a cricket's wing. I've always treated you with kindness and gave you a job. You won't go tellin' critters I'm a liar, will you?"

"Not all at, but why wouldn't you at least mention my name? Can I come with you?"

"Don't make this harder than it is, Rockford. It's time to part ways, my nutty friend."

She gave me my backpack filled with hazelnuts, thyme, salt, and popcorn kernels, then wrapped me in a big hug.

"This is horseradish! After all this time, you just go ahead and call it quits? Did I do something to upset you?"

"No, you're wonderful. Tropland evolves and changes every day! We have to listen and adapt to succeed. What do you want to do with your life?"

I looked up to the Alpine Mountains, the highest point in all of Tropland.

"You've got that look in your eye. I'd ask if you wanna go for a jog and talk it out, but I know you'll say no."

"I can't stay mad at you, Eve. Please give me fifteen minutes to warm up and stretch."

We finally went for a jog together. Needless to say, it felt good to spend one last evening with Eve, despite the buzzing and hooting from Tropland's alarming nightlife.

The next day, as we parted ways, I was faced with doubt, uncertainty, and an itchy rash on my hind leg. I had told Eve about my dream to climb the Alpines, how my curiosity to reach the unshelled diamonds as a child had become my destiny. She called me a nutty nut and said it was impossible. Eve told me I should go find my family, apologize for the past, and make amends. I missed my mother with all my heart, but I wasn't going back to my father when I knew he'd only treat me with disrespect.

Curiosity is an extraordinary ingredient in our lives. It can lead to new ideas, new friends, and to the orchids hidden deep in the swamp.

One paw after another, I was off to the great Alpine mountains! That is, after purchasing anti-itch cream, a small first-aid kit, and extra paw soap. After all, an adventure without proper hygiene is a disaster waiting to happen.

CHAPTER 7
CLIMBING FOR DESTINY

-Back to Green-Hut Market 39-

Momo, head of security, stands up on the table. He is a short and stubby orangutan with an orange tie and messy hair. Nervously shaking, he takes a deep breath and shouts toward the crowd.

"I'm sorry to say that we're having technical problems, but we should have it resolved in an hour or two. Maybe three. Possibly four, but no longer than five. Everyone in line will get two free strawberries for the inconvenience. If you decide to leave, place your baskets aside and we will put your items back where they belong. Thank you."

More and more animals show up, huddling around Rockford and Theo.

"Nobody wants to leave!" a voice from the crowd shouts.

Holly flies in closer to Rockford, talking to her camera. "Over fifteen thousand of you have decided to hear Hashtag

Rockford Origin Story LIVE from Green-Hut Market 39! Apparently, some of you even decided to make your way here! Look at this crowd! Everyone say hello!"

She flies above all the animals, who cheer for the camera.

"Did you really go to the Alpines?" asks Theo.

"Did you fight mountain trolls with your bare claws, then claim unshelled diamonds for your legendary riches?" says Randy, pushing Theo out of the way.

The two boys start fighting again.

"Boys, boys," Rockford admonishes. "Would you like me to continue, or are we going to fight again?"

They stop fighting for a moment to look for Holly, who happens to be filming right above them.

They shake once again.

"Hashtag Honeypot!" shouts Randy to the camera.

"Excuse me? Hashtag Honeypots!" shouts Theo.

Rockford stands up to stretch, then gazes through the canopy toward the Alpine Mountains in the distance. Everyone looks over to the snowcapped mountains, then back to Rockford, awaiting the next part of the story. He takes a moment to brush off some dust and moss from his jacket, then sits back on the stump to continue.

--

It took eighteen and a half days to reach the base of the great Alpine Mountains. On the way, I passed through Kona Valley visiting my childhood home to pick up a few books for my new adventure. However, the entire tree was covered in moss and buzzed with the sound of a million insects. Everything had vanished. My childhood home had been taken over by the natural order of the forest. *This is why I use paw soap so often,* I thought as I stood on the edge of the thorny branch.

Getting to the mountain was no problem, as I ran mostly through flatlands or trees. Climbing proved to be a more difficult challenge for me. As I stood at the base of the massive mountain, there were no buzzing insects or howling monkeys in any direction; only the daunting sounds of ripping thunder and tumbling rocks falling from above.

The avalanche of stones and pebbles kept me from getting more than twenty steps before falling back down. After such a rocky morning, a family of two dozen gray pikas suddenly pushed me out of their way. Looking like a rabbit and a guinea pig combined, they were walking in a single-file line.

"Excuse us."

"Pardon."

"Excuse me."

"Pardon us."

"Move it!"

Apparently, in the vast mountain range of the Alpines, I was standing precisely in their way!

Over the next month, I traveled up the mountain behind them. The trick was to hike slowly and zig-zag upwards. By slow, I mean slower than a sleeping turtle. I ran as fast as lightning on flat land, now I was moving at a snail's pace with the most sarcastic group I'd ever met. Each time I tripped up or fell, they would laugh out loud in their annoying yet adorable giggles.

"Psst! You need balance to climb. Single-file formation, chipper," said the largest of the male pikas, giving me several tiny eucalyptus sticks. "Hold these tight to prevent you from falling."

The trees looked different the higher we climbed. They were close together, with pointy, sharp leaves. I saw my breath in the air from sunrise to sunset as we hiked through a thin layer of wet clouds. The rocks felt harder and colder with every step. The temperature in the air dropped as each day passed, and still I had no clue what to do with these sticks.

After another week, we reached their destination: a small, cozy hut built inside a cave.

"Good luck, chipper. Big teeth up here," said a female pika. "Not safe for pikas. Definitely not safe for chippers."

"Wait? What do you mean by big teeth?" I asked fearfully.

"Big teeth! Big teeth!" The male pika snatched the sticks from me. "Thanks for carrying me sticks! Toodle-oo!"

I knew those weren't walking sticks.

After I split away from the pikas, it only took me a few more days to reach a large patch of green grass halfway up the mountain. The higher I climbed, the colder the grass started feeling. From there, it became damp, then wet. Suddenly, each step was more slippery, and a vast white glaze of snow covered the mountain floor. A thick, scary layer of gray fog was looming above me.

Both nervous and exited, I screamed as loud as I could.

"Heyooo!"

My voice echoed throughout the mountain range.

Heyooo... Heyooo... Heyooo... Heyooo.

For a brief moment, I felt happy. Then, spooky sounds of large animals growling surrounded me in all directions. The Alpines had no plans to keep me in a good mood.

Roars, growls, and even chuffs echoed from the distance.

Big teeth?

I dug a deep hole under a large black rock for warmth and safety that evening. After stress eating three roasted hazelnuts, I fell asleep knowing I was somewhat safe from whatever lurked in the fog.

When I woke up the next morning, I emerged from the ground well rested, but couldn't see anything but dark gray fog. I could barely see my own paws!

I scampered to my right, only to feel lost in an endless gray loop.

There was no escaping the infinite fog no matter which direction I ran!

A scary roar vibrated through my entire body.

My heart skipped a beat.

Jaguars are close.

Another roar shook the pebbles under my paws.

"Code red," I muttered under my breath, shivering with panic.

The spine-chilling roars become louder and louder. It sounded like a fight, but I couldn't see a thing!

Time to dig!

My only hope was to not get accidentally stomped on while digging my way to safety.

The fight didn't last very long. I heard the loud thumps of bodies falling, accompanied by cries and whimpers. There was a moment of silence, then the sounds of jaguars yelping as they trotted away.

What could be big enough to scare Jaguars away?

Panthers?

Bears??

Dragons???

I couldn't breathe.

From the gray fog, the dark silhouettes of five small rodents looked down upon me. They looked like floating shadows.

"Can you gallop?" a deep, mysterious voice asked.

"Should I?" I squeaked in response.

"Can you climb?" another male asked, lifting me up from

the ground.

"In this fog?"

"Give me your bag!" This voice was female.

They took the bag faster than I could blink.

"Lift your arms. Time to go!" commanded the female.

A rope was wrapped around my body. A small paw with a mighty grip grabbed my leg and smeared a type of jelly on my hind paw pads. It tickled and smelled like papaya.

"We are tied together. As one," said the voice.

"Is this sanitary?" I whimpered as the rope snapped me forward with a sudden pull.

I was tied to them as we climbed up through the endless gray fog. With each step, I felt the snap of the rope pulling me faster. I could feel the jelly on my feet gently sticking to ice, giving me much more friction to gallop as we trekked for hours on end.

"Where are we going?" I asked several times, but nobody answered.

It was a good thing I had stamina, because we just kept running! We took short rest breaks every five hours, and I slept like a koala.

The dark fog was never-ending.

"Please, I need to know one thing," I pleaded when we'd been running for so long that my legs felt like old celery. My eyes were closing. "Please. Did you… did you… did you get my paw soap? I think it fell from my backpack," I said before passing out from exhaustion.

My eyes opened to a picture-perfect blue sky. I was laying on a log, floating downriver with what appeared to be five chipmunks. The sun was far too bright to see their faces.

"Am I dreaming?" I mumbled as I closed my eyes again.

I felt a tightness around my abdomen. I opened my eyes to

see I was now dangling on a cliff wall! We were climbing directly up a vertical mountain side like a group of goats.

The blood rushed directly to my noggin and I fainted. When I woke up, I was resting comfortably on a hammock in a small, gold-lined bedroom in an orange robe.

-Back to Green-Hut Market 39-

The crowd surrounding Rockford and Theo has tripled in size.

"Theo, be a silkworm and fetch me a cup of water?" Rockford asks.

Theo reluctantly hops off Rockford's shoulder toward Holly. "How many more viewers do we have now?"

"Over twenty-eight thousand folks across Tropland are watching," says Holly in high spirits. "Wait, twenty-nine thousand! Holy Tropical Tuesdays, we're thirty thousand and climbing!"

The crowd chuckles as Theo returns with two cups of water.

"Many thanks, Theo," says Rockford, grabbing both cups. He gives one to Rosalina, who looks tired. "Here you are, dear. Theo, that was deeply kind of you for thinking about our new friend."

"Thank you," she says.

"Cheers to both ears."

"Your Great-granddad is smooth," Randy tells Theo.

"Thanks, but that was MY water."

"Now, where was I?" Rockford continues, scratching his cheeks. "Ah, yes. To everyone watching online and to our new friends here at Green-Hut Market 39, wash your paws and prepare for the wisdom of the five mindful monks."

CHAPTER 8
FIVE MINDFUL MONKS

On a list of the top three most beautiful moments of my entire life, this was certainly one of them. After figuring out how to open the sliding door, I wandered into the most magnificent garden. My paws were tickled by manicured grass. The subtle scent of roses mixed with fragrant trees produced a unique smell unlike that of an ordinary forest. In fact, behind me wasn't your ordinary Tropland tree-hut either! I had entered a realm of architectural triumph where tree-huts had roofs with pointy edges painted in shades of red and orange. I'd never seen anything like this in Tropland before, nor in any book or magazine! Not even the most skillful beavers could create such impressive structures.

As I roamed through hundreds of pink, red, purple, and white roses, I passed a bamboo bucket filled with water dripping from a pipe. With each drip, an echoed *PLINK* sounded with a soothing rhythm. I continued across a small red bridge above a freshwater pond where eight beautiful green lily pads floated on the surface.

There were dozens of small white birds inspecting every inch of the gardens, picking at imperfections in the ground and clipping the bushes with their yellow beaks. Known as cattle egret, I later learned these birds have been trusted for centuries to keep the gardens clean within the surrounding red walls.

In the distance, beyond the garden, were massive waterfalls and mountains. It was safe to say I was in the middle of nowhere. Now, this was a perfect, peaceful palace! A clean, sanitary environment with no deafening howler monkeys nor buzzing insects. It was a delight for my eyes, a gift for my nostrils, and bliss for my eardrums.

"Rockford T. Honeypot. Welcome to Eight Poem Garden," said a deep voice.

Startled, I slipped off a tree into a manicured bush.

Five golden-brown chipmunks in glistening orange robes stood over me. Each had dark green eyes, brownish red hair with two black stripes running from forehead to tail. All had arms folded behind their backs.

"How do you know my name?" I asked.

"You talk while asleep," said the tallest chipmunk of the group in a deep, calming voice. "My name is Chi. This is Mizu…" He gestured to the shortest chipmunk with a fierce grin and scar across his right eye. "… Ka…" The heaviest of the group, with his big potbelly. "… Fu…" Her long, beautiful eyelashes revealed a menacing stare. "… and Sora." The last was the most beautiful chipmunk I'd ever seen, with her dark red hair, oval-shaped eyes, and a striking gaze that left me feeling frozen in time. "We heard your cry for help."

"I certainly did not cry," I protested.

"Yes, you did," said Sora. "You were in danger."

"That was you guys fighting off the jaguars?" I asked in

disbelief.

"Rockford," said Chi, taking a few steps closer to me. "You must be wondering why we brought you here."

"Actually, I'm thankful. This place is wonderful," I said. "Is that bamboo bucket for cleaning paws? I think I'm bleeding."

"How DARE you speak of the bamboo in that manner!" shouted Mizu, the smallest of the group, yet still bigger than me. "It is to drink before a ceremony of Eight Poems. What motivation does a small chipmunk have to climb the Alpine Mountains?"

"To pursue my dream."

"Does your dream involve death by falling from a mountain peak? Or being eaten by mountain predators?" asked Fu, moving in closer. She looked similar to Sora, but a bit more rough around the edges.

"No. To find an unshelled diamond."

"And these?" asked Chi, holding my bag of roasted nuts.

"Hazelnuts, sir. My father called them filberts."

"We know they are hazelnuts!" said Sora. "And his name is Chi, not sir. Do you have a family? Were you alone on your travels?"

I sighed. "I ruined the family business. They left me two years ago in a rather dramatic fashion, I might add."

They whispered amongst themselves for a moment.

Ka stepped forward. "It has been decided. You will stay with us for one year's time." He pointed to the mountain cliff with numerous waterfalls. "There is exit if you wish to leave. We are last five remaining descendants of Tamias Aristus, mindful chip-monks. I am sorry for abandonment of your family. We know pain of loneliness. You are first outside Tamias Aristus bloodline to step paw on Eight Poem Garden for long time. Chi, our mightiest warrior, believe in prophecy of sixth mindful monk. A strong and powerful chipmunk to follow in our light. I do not see you as strong nor powerful, but we shall find out soon enough. Sora is pure of heart, but do not underestimate her strength. Triumph, and you will learn. Fail, and you must leave. Mizu and Fu are under Aristus combat training. A warning of fire: maintain distance or feel heat. Now, answer question." He held up a roasted hazelnut to his nose as his whiskers twitched. "How did you make this?"

They all seemed to tilt toward me.

"Oh, dear… umm… We call it roasting," I said, tripping backward again into the bushes. I screamed as several thorns stuck to my body. "Oh dear, now I'm definitely bleeding! I have a small first-aid kit in my bag. Can you please pass my soap and some warm water? Wait. My soap! Where's my soap?"

"This is who you believe will fulfill the prophecy?" Sora mocked, crossing her arms. "Watch your step, egghead," she growled without offering to help me up, then pivoted and walked away.

I was perplexed. Was this a dream or a nightmare? On one paw, Eight Poem Garden was flawless—a perfect palace! On the other, I was without my favorite paw soap, and doubted I could fulfill a century-old prophecy with muddy paws.

CHAPTER 9
DISCOVERING ROCKFORD

At first, it was rather difficult cohabitating with these new friends of mine. Despite being of the same species, they were much bigger, stronger, and faster than me. I shared little interest in their fighting methods or battles at the sacred fighting grounds.

"Rockford! Step into the temple and I shall teach you the sacred art of Aristus combat," shouted Mizu as he approached me in the garden one day.

"To teach implies you actually know how to fight!" Fu shouted from a distance. She charged at Mizu, knocking him over with her shoulder. Naturally, I leapt away from the action.

In moments, they were punching, kicking, spinning, and pushing. They were knocking over branches like a pair of dancing baboons.

"You act tough, but you're full of cold air!" Fu shouted, jumping high up in the air and dropping her knee toward Mizu's head.

He dodged her just in the nick of time.

I could feel my heart racing. I was certainly not cut out for this type of physical activity. My shoulders and knees would dislocate at every punch or kick! Panic flooded my mind to the point where I became nauseous.

I ran back to my tree-hut as quickly as my legs could move.

While I appreciated the mindful monks for taking me in as family, I spent the first few months with Ringo, one of the cattle egrets tending the gardens, rather than being in the middle of such physical combat.

The monks didn't seem to mind my absence as long as I helped with chores. My new garden friends, who smelled like fresh honeysuckle with hints of citrus, were very calm and peaceful. Ringo taught me to inspect, cut, and clean the grass. He later tasked me with purifying the ponds, polishing the tree-huts, trimming the trees and shrubs, removing weeds, and keeping the gardens healthy.

"Sweet like cherries. Brush like fog. Move through the whistles, scrub each log," Ringo used to repeat all day.

"Is that one of the eight poems in Eight Poem Garden?" I asked from time to time.

He would repeat himself throughout the day, every day. He never said anything else.

While caring for their sacred plants and flowers was a profound learning experience, it was also a rather prickly one. Fertilizer and mud got stuck in my nails. I was allergic to nearly everything in sight. I kept sneezing and was plagued by watery eyes. Worst of all, my paw soap was still missing!

How could a group of enlightened chipmunks lack daily hygiene such as paw soap?

"Well if it isn't the 'sixth mindful monk.' I hear you don't like getting your paws dirty," Sora mocked as she approached me on a cold afternoon. "Come with me. I'd like to show you something."

We walked to the other side of the gardens, toward some rather unusual tree-huts. Made of wood and glass, they seemed to magically sprout from the soil. Inside, a kaleidoscope of fresh fruits and vegetables grew from end to end.

"Are these your tree-huts?" I asked.

"These are more than simple tree-huts. These are green-huts. Inside, we can control the temperature and humidity to grow food all year round."

As we arrived at the magnificent structures, I could hardly believe my eyes. I'd never thought growing food out of season was possible!

SMACK!

I pulled away from the glass wall, noticing the imprint of my nose on the window.

Sora fell to her knees laughing so hard, she emitted a hog-like snort.

She tossed a handkerchief my way. "Wipe that smudge. We keep things clean around here."

I complied instantly. "With pleasure. If you're so clean, why no paw soap?"

"We have plenty. Just not for you." She grinned.

"May I ask you a question?" I said.

"Is it about soap?"

"Yes. I'm not accusing you of stealing, but Red's Paw Soap… it was in my bag. Do you know where it may have gone?"

"Oh boy, you've got a lot to learn," she said, walking inside the large green-hut filled with succulent fruits and vegetables. "Why would we steal your belongings? Look around. We have everything we need."

I was in awe. "Grapes, peaches, cucumbers in the winter? How?"

"How about sweet potatoes, kiwi, and pomegranate in the summer?" She smiled.

"The thought of eating fruits and vegetables all year makes my cheeks tingle," I gasped, wiping some drool from my lips. "Seriously, how is it possible?"

"You'll learn," Sora replied. "Ringo tells us you enjoy looking after the vegetation but are timid with elements such as dirt and soil."

"The number of bacteria in a single drop can cause severe skin problems or infertility, and don't get me started with stomach or intestinal issues."

She tossed me a pair of orange gloves. "Wear these. Now you can get your paws dirty without, you know, getting your paws dirty."

I examined the gloves carefully. "Are there any bugs in these?"

"Why would I give you gloves with bugs in them?" Sora demanded, then her face softened. "May I ask you something personal?"

"Anything. I'm an open book. Sort of. To be honest, I've never been in a relationship. Is that what you meant by personal? Oh, dear. Should I be nervous? Why am I nervous?" I couldn't stop rambling.

How embarrassing.

"Why are you so afraid?" she asked.

"Of what?"

"Everything."

"I'm not afraid. I'm just cautious."

"Against the odds, we found you in a place you don't belong. Then, for some reason, my family believes in you. And yet, as I watched you over the months, I can see you're haunted with odd fears at every blink. If you think you're an open book, tell me, why are you so afraid?"

"I'm not afraid. Being cautious keeps me safe. I got here, didn't I?"

"That's a terrible excuse! You're dodging my question. Or maybe you don't know your truth? Please sit down; I'd like to share a story with you."

"I love a good story. Can we sit over there? There's a swarm of ants on this log."

"Sit! The ants will mind their own business. When I was young, Ka told me a story about a baby tiger who was separated from his family at a very early age. He was lost wandering the forest for days without food or water. He stumbled across a herd of llamas who knew this baby tiger was no threat. They cared for him by treating him as their own, feeding him and nurturing him as part of their herd. The tiger grew up believing he was a llama and did everything a llama does—hopping around, grazing on foraged food and plants. At a time before the 'Laws of the Forest,' survival was the chief priority. None of the other llamas told the tiger the truth: that he was, in fact, a tiger. Why share the truth now that the herd was safe from predators? What animal would attack a herd with a tiger?

One day, the herd came across a pride of tigers enjoying the meat of their latest kill. He was frightened by them in the distance, but admired their strength and size. 'Who are they?' the tiger asked. 'Those are tigers,' the llamas replied. 'Stay away from them. They are the kings of the jungle and are feared by all.' Suddenly, one of the tigers let out a loud roar that shook the trees. The llamas fled to safety, and from then on, they kept their distance from predators big and small.

With each passing day, the tiger wanted to run faster than

his family, but kept calm and walked slowly with the herd. The tiger had overwhelming urges to ROAR like the king of the jungle he once saw, but kept this energy buried beneath his inner self in fear that his family would be frightened—or worse, that they would not love him for his true identity. The tiger lived the rest of his life with the llamas and passed away as an old llama. Rockford, do you know why I'm telling you this story?"

"Truthfully, I heard every word, but I've also been eyeing the swarm of ants getting closer to my leg."

"Don't be so afraid of every small twist and turn in life! The tiger ignored the roar of his inner self. No matter what happens or how long you spend with us, never underestimate what you're capable of doing."

She gave me a kiss on the cheek and tossed me a stone.

"My purple amethyst! I thought I had lost it."

"Don't grow old thinking you're a llama when deep down, you know you're a tiger."

This was the first time in my life that I questioned my identity. *I was Captain Rockford T. on a mission of adventure, right?* Or was I making a huge mistake by staying with chipmunks in orange pajamas?

I had plenty of time to think about the meaning of Sora's story during the following changing seasons. When I looked at my reflection in the still waters of the pond, the chilling fear of never seeing my family reflected back at me. Did I make the right decision to choose my own adventures, all on my own? Many sleepless nights rustled my confidence.

Captain Llama Honeypot?

Thankfully, there was one pinch of good fortune at that time: I nabbed four bars of spearmint paw soap from Sora's tree-hut. *Such a delight to have clean paws!*

-Back to Green-Hut Market 39-

Ben has been holding his arm in the air for a few minutes now.

"Yes? Do you have a question?" Rockford asks.

"Yes. So sorry to interrupt, but did you and Sora ever hook up? She literally sounds like the most amazing chipmunk. I bet she's hot."

Everyone chuckles.

"Oh, sweet Sora," Rockford sighs. "She was a very close friend of mine."

"Did Great-grandmom know Sora?" whispers Theo.

"Not personally. I met your great-grandmother later in my life."

"How many viewers?!" Randy shouts.

"Eighty thousand curious critters and counting. We're officially a Whisker sticker!" Holly replies, floating above the crowd.

"No way! We're trending on the homepage?" shouts Randy.

Theo races up Randy's tail to the top of his head. "We're trending!" he screams, flailing his arms with accomplishment.

"Oh, dear. We've got more visitors. Where was I?" Rockford asks.

"Sora's story of the llama and the tiger," Rosalina chimes in.

"Ah, yes. Thank you."

"I assume you lived like a tiger?" she asks.

"After hearing that story, I questioned my identity—something I think we should all do from time to time. If only Sora knew what I have accomplished over the years. I'm no tiger, but I am a chipmunk who listened to his roar and built an empire of wealth for a thousand generations."

"Score!" Theo shouts. "Could you buy me the velvet yo-yo with the grape-scented string?"

"Sure, if that's what you want when it's your birthday," Rockford replies, rubbing the youngster's head. "But for now, let's continue."

CHAPTER 10
ROCKFORD REDEFINED

I grew to appreciate the monks for their own unique ways. Ka, the main chef of the group, took a passionate shine to roasting. Based on the blueprint of Farley's roasting oven I had sketched in my journal, we built an upgraded 'pit' from mud and stones. Ka added his own twist with finely-tuned culinary delights. Most notably, he used coconut oil instead of olive oil, and a tray rather than a soup pot.

Everything was documented in my journal. In fact, I wrote about every sight, sound, smell, and bite-sized nugget of wisdom experienced during my time with the monks. They were such a welcoming, semi-friendly group. Except for Mizu; I avoided him like deadly nightshade berries!

My most memorable times were with sweet Sora. She taught me the ancient language of Kern from a book called 'Light.' This was unlike any book I'd seen or read. It was wrapped in dark purple vines with a tree imprint on the green cover, as if the trees themselves had created each page with love.

"This is right up your branch," she commented as we read the first chapter. "It's a comprehensive system of philosophy, as well as art and logic."

"Am I to assume the botanical science behind the green-huts?"

"Yes. You'll love the chapter of photosynthesis, by which plants make their own food from sunshine."

It took a few months to learn; not because it was difficult, but because we were constantly interrupted by Mizu.

"Reading the Book of Light again? You don't deserve to read that book," snarled Mizu.

"Back off, Mizu," Sora snapped.

"The sun shines for everyone, does it not?" I replied.

"You have shown us great respect by sharing your ways of roasting," Mizu continued. "But to truly understand Kern, you must understand our way of life."

He swung a mighty fist toward my face, brushing my whiskers. I froze like an ice cube.

"Mizu!" Sora yelled at him.

"He can't fight. I am the smallest of the group, yet I fight the hardest!" Mizu retaliated. "Chi believes in your heart, as does Sora. You have yet to convince me, Rockford. Why do you wish to learn about our history and tradition? What's your intention? Next month is the one-year mark since your arrival, and you have yet to fight me!"

I was terrified once again by his pushy tone.

"I'm not going to tell you again." Sora bared her teeth and stood before Mizu, using her entire body as a shield.

"Sunflower seeds!" I shrieked.

Sora looked confused. "What?"

"Anyone want some roasted sunflower seeds?" I tried to walk away. "Or… roasted almonds?"

"I have a better idea!" Mizu took a few steps closer to me.

Sora grabbed his shoulder and twisted him around before he could do anything else.

The two tried to exchange punches for a few moments while I stayed out of the way. Not a single punch landed, however; they both were too fast for each other.

Sora's grace was mesmerizing. Even the way she punched and kicked looked beautiful—especially when Mizu was on the ground with Sora's hind paw pressed up against his neck.

"You want to fight him? Train him first! Tomorrow at sunrise in the temple," she yelled.

"Fine. Get off!" he yelled back.

"Train who? Wait. Me?" I asked.

Sora helped Mizu up off the ground. "Yes, you! He's right. If you ARE a mindful monk, you act like a tiger, not a llama!"

"We'll see if this cub has claws once and for all," Mizu said, dusting himself off. "Tomorrow morning! Sunrise!"

I decided at that moment to do what needed to be done. It was the only way to diffuse the situation and stop this nonsense once and for all.

Sprint as fast as possible in the opposite direction!

For the next month, I stayed near the cattle egrets, looking after all the vegetation in the green-huts. I didn't interact with anyone except Sora, but even she was upset with me for my lack of interest in combat.

The time for the monks' decision—one year since my arrival—had finally dawned. It was a very chilly evening; the full moon was struggling to glow through the thick clouds.

All five mindful monks stood in a circle as I sat awkwardly in the middle. Small fires were lit around the garden as part of their ceremonial tradition. In front of the temple was the largest controlled fire I'd ever seen. The glow flickered across the gardens, casting ominous shadows over the monks who stared down at me in their orange robes.

"Rockford," said Chi in a serious tone. "It has been one year since your arrival. It is true that a prophecy has been written of a sixth mindful monk, born into our bloodline, returning to fulfill their destiny. You have provided us with knowledge of roasting. You have cared for our green-huts. You are an extraordinary, talented chipmunk. We are grateful for your kindness."

I felt a cold breeze on my back, adding to the anxiety building from head to tail.

Chi placed his paw on my shoulder. "But… you are not one of us. The time has come for you to leave."

"Now?" My lip started to quiver.

Ka stepped forward. "Not now. There is a storm coming this evening. When it passes, Mizu will escort you."

"It was a pleasure to know you, Rockford," Fu spoke up, "Don't be upset. You have much to look forward to in your life."

I felt an inexplicable sadness. *Why should this news warrant such emotion?* I was just a chipmunk from Kona Valley, not the answer to an ancient prophecy!

As I gazed up at the dark sky, the unshelled diamonds disappeared into the thick clouds. Perhaps this was a sign that I should return home and re-evaluate my life choices. The whole reason behind this journey had been to capture an unshelled diamond, and I hadn't attempted it once throughout the entire year!

Or perhaps it was time to admit that all my choices, no matter the adventure, would result in predictable failure.

In between blinks, I caught Sora's beautiful stare. I wanted to speak, but it felt like a tadpole was swimming down my throat.

"LOOK OUT!" screamed Sora.

A large tree branch flew toward us. Everyone leapt out of the way except me. For that brief moment, I froze up with fear.

THUD!

Sora tackled me, preventing me from being mashed like a sweet potato.

"Oh dear!" I gasped. My paws were trembling. "Sora, you saved my life!"

"The wind is picking up. Get to the temple!" shouted Mizu.

Sora and I tried to catch up with the group, dodging rocks, branches, and debris from all angles. To make matters worse, the fires across the gardens were blowing out from the howling wind.

"We'll be swept away if we don't get to the temple!" Chi yelled.

We kept running, but the darkness was making it difficult to see. A bolt of lightning gave us a momentary glimpse of direction.

"This way!" shouted Sora. She grabbed my arm as we tried catching up to the group.

"Rockford! Be careful! The green-huts are shattering!"

The rumble of booming thunder vibrated through my entire body. My beloved green-huts were being crushed by branches. The glass was exploding outward from the force of the powerful storm.

"Protect yourselves. Get to the temple!" shouted Fu.

'ROCKFORD!" Sora screamed.

Her face went pale with pain as she dropped to the ground. I looked down in horror to see that she had a piece of glass lodged in her thigh, bleeding heavily.

"SORA!" I reached out for her paw, but her sudden stillness

allowed the winds to push her around like a leaf.

"Sora, grab my paw! GRAB MY PAW!"

I reached out as far as my arm could stretch! The wind was taking Sora away from me. With her last heroic effort, she leapt toward me and gripped my tail. I started digging forcefully into the ground, Sora hanging on to my tail, floating up into the wind.

"Rockford!"

Once I'd dug deep enough to avoid the strongest gusts of wind, I pulled Sora in closer.

"Dig with me!" I shouted.

We continued digging until we were immersed in near darkness.

My heart was racing. "Sora, are you okay?"

She tore a small piece of robe off her arm. "I'll be fine. Pain is only as strong as the attention we give to it."

I helped her wrap it tightly around her injured leg.

For the moment, we were safe.

"Thank you," she whispered, just before falling asleep against my shoulder.

"Thank you," I whispered back, feeling her breath brushing the side of my cheek.

I took a deep breath.

"Thank you."

CHAPTER 11
SIXTH MINDFUL MONK

Back to Green-Hut Market 39-

The crowd is considerably larger, as more animals continue to arrive. The livestream is going viral across the forest to every species of all ages. From monkeys and pigs to ducks and mice, the word is spreading about Rockford's Origin Story.

"Did you make it out safely?" Randy asks, hopping back on his tail.

"Obviously! He's here telling the story, isn't he?" replies Theo, folding his arms in disgust.

"I wasn't talking to you!" Randy shouts, throwing a few peanuts at Theo.

An older chipmunk from the crowd speaks up. "Enough already! We're trying to listen, and you two won't stop squawking the whole wooly time!" He is dressed in a snazzy brown suit, brown tie, and brown shoes; his daughter, wearing dark green jeans and a turquoise tank top, stands next to him. "Mr. Honeypot, the name is Douglas Waterloo. This is my daughter, Ann. We'd like to hear more about your time with the mindful monks and their ancient wisdom. It's both fascinating and rare to hear insight from an accomplished business executive like yourself."

"What? No, we don't," grumbles Ann. "Mr. Honeypot, were you and Sora an item?"

"Hey now!" Douglas admonishes. "I didn't raise you to speak like that. Apologize right now, Ann!"

"Sorry for being interested in love," she mumbles before being bumped aside by a dozen animals approaching from the golden checkout line. The rude group pushes everyone out of their way in order to gain the best view.

"Excuse me. Do you need anything?" Rockford asks the red fox leading the commotion.

The fox sits near Rockford. His designer suit is perfect in every way. "A lemonade would be ideal. Don't mind us," he says, flicking Theo's yo-yo off the tree-stump.

"What the fruit stand?" says Theo, picking up his yo-yo.

"It's a cheap toy, sport. Get over it," says the fox. "We came for the story. Do continue."

Randy notices Theo's whimper as he stands in fear of the angry fox. He bounces up on his tail, towering above the rude stranger. "Beat it, *sport*!"

"Know your place!" replies the fox, tail pointed up. "Rockford, how about you join our… how do I put it? Our more *sophisticated* section across the marketplace?"

"That tone is unwanted like fungus." Rockford pushes his glasses back up onto his nose. "If you'd like to listen to the story, we're livestreaming it, so please watch from the comfort of your *sophisticated* section."

The crowd cheers once again. Randy and Theo point toward the exit line. The rude group shuffles away, annoyed.

"That was fresh, Mr. Honeypot," Ann says, dusting herself off from a distance. "I hope I didn't offend you."

"I'm not easily offended in my old age," Rockford assures her amiably. "Especially when my great-grandson looks at you with that twinkle."

"What? Great-granddad!" Theo shouts, putting his paws over his head in embarrassment.

Rockford waves to Ann with a smile.

Theo's cheeks turn tomato-red as he tries to hide behind his Great-grandfather.

"Back to the story, shall we?"

--

Sora and I remained underground for two days until the storm had completely passed. When we surfaced, we couldn't believe our eyes. Entire trees had been snapped, bent, and ripped apart across the garden. Brown mud replaced the once manicured green grass. The tree-huts were nowhere in sight. All that remained of their sacred temple were the eight steps by the entrance. Worst of all, my green-huts were demolished, with wood, glass, dirt, and vegetation scattered everywhere.

Eight Poem Garden was completely destroyed.

Thankfully, all five monks and the cattle egrets made it safely to the temple's underground burrow with no serious injuries.

This Honeypot doesn't abandon his friends or family when life takes a nasty turn.

I offered to stay and help the monks clean up. Despite being asked to leave before the storm, they were grateful to have an extra set of paws during this dark time. I empathized with the monks and their devastating loss. As a child, we moved tree-huts after the termites took everything from us. While a youngster, I watched as my family left me behind with nothing but hope for the future. I felt their pain and heartbreak with every whisker.

We cracked nuts in the mornings and shared hearty meals together as a family. Day by day, we cleaned up Eight Poem Garden with determination and grit. It took months just to clear the garden of all the debris. Sora then asked me to stay and help rebuild their temple as the center of the garden. It took almost a year to get both the temple and small tree-huts back to the high standards of the monks.

"Each day a journey," Ka said upon entering the new temple for the first time. "A battle of blood or heart. To live is to love."

He took a long, deep breath, then returned to work.

"Sora, is that one of the eight poems?" I whispered.

"It was the first," she said. "To me, it means we all fight battles every day, either physical or emotional. But despite the size of our problems, we're here to love. Ka must have a place for you in his heart to allow you to hear one of the eight poems."

"It's beautiful," I replied, "like you."

She leaned over, eyes locked in a grateful stare, and kissed me on the lips.

I felt my heart skip a beat as her whiskers tickled my cheeks.

"Get back to work," she said, then ran off.

I was so overwhelmed with giddy bliss, I didn't know how to react. My first kiss—and with the most incredible chipmunk I'd ever met. Best of all, I didn't have an allergic reaction!

Another year passed as Sora and I became more than friends. Plus, I started to get along with everyone! Mizu and Fu trained me in the art of Aristus combat. We spent the wee hours of the mornings on strength, coordination, balance, mobility, and self-defense. At first, it was like combining prunes with garlic; some things just don't mix. But after the first year, I developed more muscle and agility. Even with the endless physical activity and Mizu's psycho-babble, I learned to love this part of my day.

Ka and I spent time together in the early afternoons roasting, cooking, and planning meals. We had rebuilt the ovens and fire pits, created new recipes, and experimented with different roasting techniques. He loved adding cinnamon to roasted almonds and pairing them with a hot cup of mint tea.

Chi and I spent time later in the afternoons building the new and improved green-huts. They were larger than the previous models, so we needed a new system to water the vegetation. Since the garden didn't have much power, unlike Tropland, we had to be clever. By placing vines from nearby trees inside along the ceiling, rainwater was able to trickle down and drip across the plants.

Chi had stored a variety of seeds deep within the subfloor in a vault in case of just such an emergency. We replanted all throughout each green-hut. I watched in amazement as Chi turned sand into glass before my eyes. With all the knowledge they had of fire in a controlled setting, I was surprised they hadn't figured out how to roast nuts on their own! Still, the multi-colored flames and eye-watering heat were far too dangerous for me to attempt.

Finally, I spent my evenings with Sora. I was so head-over-paws with that chipmunk that I learned to be fluent in Kern by hearing her read about photosynthesis. She could have read the Tropland phone directory and I would have been captivated. Sora was my first crush, and my first love. She was the first of many new experiences in my life.

We spent hours cracking nuts and talking about everything from food pairings to pinecones. Sora taught me how to be grateful for what we had rather than what we wanted; I taught her the most efficient ways to wash paws and claws in a hurry. She told me stories filled with the wisdom of her ancestors; I told her stories filled with adventure from the Captain James T. series.

As another year came and went, we found ourselves lying on newly manicured grass one humid evening, staring up toward the night sky.

"Why do you call them unshelled diamonds? They are stars, bright bookmarks of our history," Sora said.

"They are the unshelled diamonds of possibility. Captain James T. used them to accomplish what others believed to be impossible."

"Is that what you will do? The impossible? I hate to be the one to break it to you, but those stars are way out of reach."

"You're the one who said pain is only as strong as the attention we give to it. So, it's only out of reach if we believe it's out of reach."

She tackled me to the ground and pinned me down. Despite my best efforts, Sora was too strong. She buried me up to my neck in the dirt and sat on top of my body.

"You, Rockford T. Honeypot, are full of charm, aren't you?"

"Let me out! The dirt is moist and full of worms!" I yelped.

"Are you gonna wait your whole life for an unshelled diamond, or are you gonna take it?"

"I'm gonna take it!"

"When?"

"I don't know. Gross! Caterpillar!" I could feel the slimy

creature climbing up my shorts.

"Things happen for a reason when the time is right," she stated.

"A lesson? Now? Just let me out!"

"Rockford. Be calm for ten seconds!"

I blew out an irritated breath. "Fine."

"Time is brittle wind. Stars shine with each passing gust. Will you be ready?" she asked.

"Is that another Eight Poem… poem?"

"Yes. What does it mean to you?"

"I'm not sure. Perhaps that time is passing, and we should be ready for anything?"

"I like that." She finally stood up and helped me out of the dirt. "To me, it means that things happen when they are supposed to happen. Divine timing. Can I share a secret with you?"

"You can share anything with me."

"I'm not feeling too good lately, Rockford," she mumbled, looking toward the stars.

"Sick? As in contagious?" I said, scooting back.

"No. But soon I may fall ill. I want you to remember me like I am today."

Her words shocked me.

A tear fell from my cheek. "I can help. How did this happen? I'll do anything! I'm here for you."

"There is a place in the east with healing spring waters. We will travel there as a family, and I promise I will be healthy."

"When do we leave?"

"You can't come with us. Chi won't let anyone but Tamias Aristus on the journey. I appreciate your love. I feel it. We met for a reason, and one day, when the timing is right, we'll meet again. Have faith in us, please. Can you do me a favor?"

"Anything for you."

"Live a life worth living."

Our eyes locked together in a deep embrace. I was overwhelmed with extreme love and loss, a tender combination.

I asked if I could join her a thousand times over the next month with no luck. I'd felt a thousand nuts crack in my life, but never the pain of a cracked heart.

It was springtime. Beautiful, bright blue skies and a brighter white sun shone on the semi-restored Eight Poem Garden. The flowers were in full bloom that morning, yet I only felt sadness.

Sora was inside the temple with a fever.

I sat on the steps, waiting to see her.

"Rockford," Chi spoke up. "We have endured and embraced change in the harshest conditions."

"Sora. Tell me about Sora. Please. Will she be alright?"

"Yes, she will. You may not be a direct descendant of Tamias Aristus, but you have the heart of a mindful monk. Tomorrow, we will take Sora east to the ancient ruins of our ancestors, where she'll heal. If you wish to say goodbye, now is the time."

Still holding back tears, I nodded my head and walked inside the temple. Small orange candles surrounded the bed where Sora was resting.

"Rockford?" she whispered.

"It's me. You feeling any better?"

"Yes. I am strong. You are a good chipmunk, Rockford T. Honeypot. Will you pray with me?"

"I've never prayed before," I whispered, "but before we begin, I have to be honest and tell you that I stole four bars of your paw soap. I'm sorry."

"Give me that clean paw, silly." She held her paw toward mine with a smile. "Take a deep breath. Be mindful of your breath and close your eyes. Imagine a force that guides the wind, chills the waters, and reflects the shiny unshelled diamonds in the night sky. This force grants us the beauty of our trees, flowers, fruits, vegetables, and life itself. Take a deep breath with me. Do you feel the wind on your whiskers? Breathe this force into your body as energy. We ask this force to guide us through the river of joy, love, gratitude, peace, and harmony. We ask for our strength and for protection over those we love dear."

"That's beautiful, Sora," I said, feeling the back of my neck tingle with emotion. "Can I breathe out yet?"

"You weren't supposed to hold your breath this whole time." She laughed then coughed a few times. Sora gave me a small box wrapped in a purple vine. "I'm sorry you can't travel with us. Don't give up, Captain Rockford T. Don't lose that curiosity of yours, either. I promise I will be healed."

I couldn't hold back the tears now. I wept like a jungle puppy.

"Mizu and Fu will escort you down to where we found you by the black rock. There, you will be on your own," said Chi.

I kissed Sora on the forehead one last time.

"Come!" Ka entered the room. "Can't leave on empty stomach. Breakfast is waiting."

It was a sad conclusion to this chapter in my life—a chapter I didn't want to end. I'll never forget the love, compassion, and gratitude I was shown by the mindful monks during our time together. In my heart I knew that Sora would be healthy, happy, and strong.

As we were leaving, I snuck a letter inside my favorite green-hut.

To Eight Poem Garden,

Thank you for keeping my belly full and allowing me to help restore your beauty. Your lessons will forever be a part of my journey.

Cheers to both ears,
Rockford T. Honeypot

CHAPTER 12

THE FLYING CHIPMUNKS

When I left Eight Poem Garden, the monks put an orange blindfold over my eyes. Mizu and Fu led me to the black rock where we first met years before. As agreed, I unfortunately had to exchange my orange robe for the clothes I was wearing way back then. Over that time, I had grown much bigger and stronger. Now, I looked ridiculous in my old Evening Musk uniform.

Shortly after we parted ways, I couldn't resist the temptation to open Sora's gift.

I unwrapped the purple vine with great anticipation, then gently peeled back the grape leaf to find a shiny stone.

I couldn't believe my eyes!

I was holding an unshelled diamond in my paw!

It reflected the colors of the rainbow across my face, sparkling like the night sky.

Inside was a small handwritten note from Sora:

Dearest Rockford,

You light up my heart. Keep shining.

Love, Sora

My whole life I had dreamed of this moment! I held the diamond close to my heart, *but why did I feel as empty as a duck's nest?* I would have traded it faster than a lightning bolt for a chance to see Sora again. So many questions mixed with a million emotions made sleeping difficult for weeks.

I wandered into a town called Westwoods late one evening. Much like the bigger towns of Tropland, tunnels, bridges, and vines connected this lively community. On that particular evening the Crabapple Carnival was in full bloom. Every hut in town had live music playing louder than the next where animals wearing dark red wigs danced the night away.

A few baboons and prairie dogs stumbled away from the street parade in my direction. I hid the diamond in my backpack.

"Crabapple Carnival! Oooga, baby!" one of the baboons shouted. "Isn't this one adorable? Come with us, honey."

"It's Honeypot," I quietly corrected him.

I followed them through the parade of animals to a hut called Magpies Chatter, which we had to wait in a long line to enter.

"Rockford!" shouted a voice from the front of the line. "Rockford! Rockford!"

It was hard to see, but way up in the distance was Joel, the harvest mouse I met when I first left Kona Valley.

"Joel! How lovely to see a familiar face." I ran to him, smiling for the first time in a long while. "Where's the rest of the group?"

"Our band, The Mischiefs, are inside. Look at you, mate! You're three times bigger than I remember. Been working out much? Well, don't stand there like a candlestick. Have a crabapple and join us!"

We walked in to the bright lights of Magpies Chatter.

"This hut is filthy. What brought you here?" I asked.

"Filthy? You've got it upside down with your foul stench, mate. This is Westwoods City! The best town for music, eats, and the finest fermented crabapples in all of Tropland."

"What's a fermented crabapple?" I asked.

"Less talk, more action. Let's find you some clothes that fit!" he shouted.

That night was also my first experience eating crabapples, fermented over time to have all the same attributes as an alcoholic beverage. The Mischiefs played their music loud enough to make my eardrums whistle.

After my second crabapple, I felt free, peaceful, and a touch dizzy. Joel was kind enough to find me loose-fitting clothes meant for a small monkey. My backpack was safe with The Mischiefs' equipment, it was time to let loose and dance! My Tamias Aristus training allowed me to strut my stuff with other chipmunks, beavers, shrews, foxes, salamanders, squirrels, and a white-tailed deer fawn on the dance floor. Finally, a moment of happiness!

"One half crabapple, my fellow chordate!" I mumbled to the bartender, a mouse with a top hat and a twirly mustache.

"What did you just call me?"

"Chordate," I explained, my words slurring slightly, "belonging to the phylum Chordata. Come on, how do you not know the classifications of your own species?"

"Know your limits, chipmunk. One more, and that's it for the evening."

"Aye, aye!" I stuttered with a hiccup. "Wait. Is that my bag? Hey! That's my bag!"

A beefy muskrat wearing a brown jacket was walking out

the back door with my backpack.

"That's my bag, you oaf! That's my bag!" I yelled, chasing after him. When I caught up with the muskrat outside, I snatched my bag from his paw.

"What the deuce do you think you're doing, you drunk?" shouted the muskrat.

"I should ask you the same question, you brute! You think you can steal from Captain James T. Rockford Honeypot?"

As I inspected the bag, I noticed pink vine wrapped around the zipper.

"Eh?" I mumbled.

SMACK!

A female red squirrel smacked the back of my head and took the bag from me.

"That's for stealing my bag, ya dill-witted buffoon," she yelled.

Despite the tension in the air, I giggled. No one had ever called me a dill-witted buffoon before.

"Why don't you wait for us inside, Betty? We'll handle this," growled the muskrat. He took off his jacket and threw it on a branch.

Four palm squirrels stood behind me, itching for a fight.

"Hurry up, boys. Mamma wants to dance," Betty said, walking back inside. "Make sure he learns from his mistake."

"Don't worry, Betty baby. We'll make sure this mouse crawls back to his hole," replied one of the squirrels.

"I eat corn husks bigger than you," snarled one of the bigger squirrels, approaching me.

"I can tell," I said with a hiccup.

His beady eyes were fixed on me with predatory anger. Without hesitation, I entered combat mode, punching him square between the legs.

"Oh! Sucker punch to the tassel berries!" shouted the hefty muskrat.

I felt another paw grab my shoulder. Time froze like an icicle, but flashbacks of training with Fu and Mizu flooded my muscles with energy.

I flipped over the squirrel and threw him through the back door of Magpies Chatter. The loud music behind me felt like a second pulse, pumping through my racing heart. Maybe it was because of the crabapples, but I suddenly had never felt more alive!

The other three squirrels were no match. One by one, I tossed them aside harnessing the energy of Aristus combat. I may as well have been fighting dandelions floating in the air! After a few minutes, I had thrown each of them four branches up in the tree. They twirled slowly by their tails like a bunch of bananas, too tired to continue.

The muskrat approached me, paws in the air. "Whoa there, gladiator. The name's Chuck. This fell from your pockets." He held my amethyst stone and tossed it my way. "Listen, I'm sorry about earlier. Betty's the boss around here… I don't like her much. You hear the way she yells? How about a crabapple, and you tell me where you learned to fight like that?"

Chuck Goldblum turned out to be one of the most highly-trained muskrats in the Alpine Mission Force (AMF). Although Chuck was large and intimidating, he had the heart of a loyal friend as well as the strange scent of cinnamon leaves. He let me stay with him for a few weeks, hoping I'd teach him Aristus combat. From the couches to the tables, I felt tiny in his extra-large tree-hut. On the flip side, sleeping on his cinnamon-scented sofa was a treat!

With no job or other source of income, my options to be able to afford food and everyday necessities were limited.

Chuck convinced me to chip off a very small sliver of the unshelled diamond in order to live comfortably. I was now able to buy new well-fitting clothes and rent my own tree-hut six branches above him. I even bought a snazzy purple jacket and matching trousers that Sora would have appreciated. At this rate, my unshelled diamond would bring me a lifetime of ease.

If only Sora were with me.

Chuck spent months begging me to teach him Tamias Aristus combat. His appreciation and desire to master the intricate fighting style grew stronger and stronger. One morning, while we were enjoying a cup of hazelnut coffee, he finally won me over.

"Chuck, do you want one or two drops of sugar?" I asked while ordering at Hubert's Beans, a local favorite in Westwoods. It was built high in the canopy with tables and sofas comfortably arranged throughout.

"Just a shake of cinnamon, Rocky!" he replied. "I've been thinking. Back in the AMF, we kept things very private. No inside secrets left our band of kettles."

"Here you are. One cup of java, one shake of cinnamon." I joined him at the table.

"Thanks! A kettle is a group of hawks, by the way," he said, sipping his coffee.

"Yes, I know. And I stay away from them. Along with bacteria, fungus, and termites."

"We were the best of the bestest in the AMF," Chuck continued. "The only group who dared to hawk-glide. We could travel hundreds of times farther and faster than any transport goose in the forest. You teach me the Tamias Aristus fighting style, and I'll show you how to hawk-glide. That's a fair trade. One ancient secret for another."

"It does sound like a Captain James T. adventure," I

conceded thoughtfully, "where he flew a scoop owl over the red river in search of Egyptian chamomile flowers. On the contrary, my mother would tell me as a child, 'You see a hawk, you gallop, don't walk!' Her cousin Erica was snatched up by a hawk when she was a young pup. I've been terrified of them since hearing of her misfortune."

Chuck snorted. "You have nothing to be afraid of with me as your guide. Besides, you think too much. It'll change your life! Trust Chuck."

The day I jumped on the back of a giant hawk was one of the scariest moments of my life. It was a hot afternoon, and the heavy, earthy scent of sequoia scones made my eyes water. Chuck and I stood at the bottom of an enormous tree. I had packed new paw soap and a first aid kit along with my usual travel accessories in my backpack.

"First, we need to spot the great hawks. That can be tricky," Chuck explained. "Neither the gray-lined hawk nor roadside hawk have the wingspan we need. We prefer the biggest, baddest raptor in the jungle: the great black hawk. Make sure its eyes are dark as the night. The scarier it looks, the faster it flies. Luckily for us, you're an easy target! Just run around in circles and wait for them to notice. Ready?"

"Absolutely not!" I shrieked. "Are you nuts?"

"Crazy as a cashew! Did I forget to mention, you'll be running around a small fire? It'll be fun!"

"Excuse me? Do you have a fire license?"

He shrugged. "Hawks are very smart and are natural hunters. They don't abide by Tropland's rules, and the police can't catch 'em. Once they spot the gray smoke from our fire, they'll perch on a tree and wait for the moment to strike. Don't worry, that's when we'll blow the fire out! The gray smoke will turn dark black and distract the hawk. That's when we'll race up behind it."

I folded my arms. "These are the actions of a bandit, of which I will exclude myself from such activities."

"Live a little! I've done this a thousand times."

Live a little? Sora had wanted me to live a life worth living.

"Trust Chuck, remember?" he continued. "Make sure that stone of yours stays in your pocket this time."

With extreme hesitation on my part, we followed his plan carefully until the smoke caught the attention of a large black hawk. Throwing a few rocks over the pit extinguished the fire, causing thick black smoke to blanket the upper layer of the forest canopy.

We climbed up the tree toward the great beast. I was struggling to catch my breath by the time we reached the top. That's where I caught my first glimpse of the hawk. The fierce creature was the size of a hundred chipmunks, with the sharpest claws I'd ever seen!

We got in position, ready to take a leap of faith.

"On the count of three," Chuck whispered. "I'll count."

My heart was thumping.

"One…"

"Wait. I'm too nervous," I mumbled.

"Two…"

"Hold it. I've changed my mind."

Chuck pulled a pair of goggles from his inside pocket and placed them over his eyes. Without another word, he gripped my arm and jumped off the branch.

We landed perfectly on the neck of the beast! The hawk snapped his head up and took to the air.

"What happened to three?!" I shouted.

"We're flying!" he shouted back.

I held on to a feather with all my might, squinting my eyes

to shield myself from the piercing wind. The next few moments were life-changing. There we were, two rodents flying high through the canopy, whirling above the clouds, defying the natural laws of the forest. The slow and steady speed of a transport goose couldn't compare to the rapid acceleration of a great black hawk!

We stayed on that hawk for over an hour, gliding through the air. The wind was zipping past us faster than a storm in mid-April.

"How do you make him stop?" I yelled.

"It's easy!" Chuck screamed. "Since we can't speak hawk, just lick your finger and stick it in his ear!"

I couldn't tell if he was joking or not.

Sure enough, that's exactly what he did. The hawk shook its head and dipped down at full-speed through the
plant crowns onto a branch, and we leapt off.

I kissed the ground once we made it down safely. Nothing is better than having your paws on the sod. As I looked up, I realized I had no idea where we were in Tropland. My stomach was twisted from all the excitement.

"Time for lunch. Flying makes me hungry!" Chuck declared.

CHAPTER 13
THE CROWN JEWEL

-Back to Green-Hut Market 39-

Sitting next to Rockford, Randy's eyes are wide open, his pupils dilated with excitement. He tugs on Rockford's jacket. "My grandmother taught me the sacred art of croquet. I'll swap her ancient secrets if you teach me to hawk-glide or Tamias combat!"

"Maybe when you're older," replies Rockford, noticing Ann staring at Theo from the crowd.

Rockford adjusts his posture. "Douglas, Ann, would you two like to come a little closer?"

"Would you look at that? We're part of the story, sweetheart," says Douglas, smiling

from cheek to cheek.

As they approach, Theo tries hiding behind Randy, but his attempt falls flat. He trips over Randy's tail into the bushes.

"Need a paw?" Ann reaches out to help him up.

"Umm. Thanks."

"Don't forget to invite me to your wedding!" Randy says, laughing.

"Rude!" shouts Theo.

"If you put your nail over the string for the first few wind-ups, it'll wind tighter," says Ann, adjusting Theo's yo-yo.

"Umm," mumbles Theo, scratching the back of his neck.

"I've been yo-yoing since I was five." She looks toward Rockford with her twinkling green eyes. "Mr. Honeypot, is this when you finally met Jewel?"

"Almost. Chuck and I spent time together hawk-gliding throughout Tropland. You might not believe it, but we had some action-packed adventures on par with Captain James T. first!"

--

Over the next two years, Chuck became, as he put it, "a brother from another mother" to me. From east to west, north to south, we flew across the forest. As premiere explorers, we used tiny pieces of my diamond to fund our experiences of Tropland's luxuries. My heart yearned to share this epic adventure and excitement with Sora and the mindful monks.

In the cold regions of Tropland's South Pole, we visited the royal penguins and their chilly city of Vetgana. In the tropical region of West Tropland, we attended galas and fundraising events with Hollygrove celebrities. East Tropland was full of wide sandy beaches that were fun to explore. We had a hoot and holler trying to keep the sand away from those hard-to-reach areas. The northernmost part of Tropland was a blissful paradise! It was filled with waterfalls, white sandy beaches, unique flowers, and the finest banana mango smoothies.

Despite our epic adventures, we failed to reach the towering heights of the Alpine Mountains. I had to finally admit that after many attempts, Eight Poem Garden will forever be out of reach, hidden by the altitude and hazy gray fog.

Upon our return to Westwoods, I rented a nice tree-hut in the hippest part of town. I only had to use a sliver of the diamond to last many months. For the first time in a long while, I felt secure in life.

Our favorite activity was going out in the evenings, making new friends and eating fermented crabapples. Chuck could eat at least five or six and still function well in society. After three, I would be dancing the Macadamia on tables, so I learned to pace myself with only one or two.

I was never very smooth with the ladies. On one paw, I was strong and handsome, with near perfect hygiene. On the other, conversing with the female gender made me freeze like sorbet. Chuck was a different story. The guy was natural catnip in the great forest.

One autumn evening, we went to Red Fox Hoolies, a lounge with a flashy neon red sign out front, and dozens of wooden fox statues lining the entrance. A long queue of animals dressed in bright colors were waiting to get in. Normally, it would have taken us a while to enter, but we bribed the bouncer with a roasted hazelnut to let us bypass the line.

This hut was very upscale, filled with ladies way out of my league.

"Authentic beauty is so rare that when you catch a glimpse, it stops you right in your paw prints," Chuck explained. "You see all these pretty squirrels and chipmunks around here?"

"Oh yes," I replied. "My paws are sweaty. Perhaps I should go wash up now."

"What? No! Don't be so nervous," he tried to reassure me.

"Here's the lesson for the evening: the gals we're looking for don't care about shiny things like unshelled diamonds or designer clothing, so don't pretend you're anyone but yourself. Beauty attracts beauty, right?"

"If you say so."

"It's like you said—how fimanuci math was beautiful in nature. It's the same thing!"

"The Fibonacci sequence?! Explain how a mathematical sequence where each number is the sum of the previous two numbers has any relevance to picking up gals in a bar?"

"I mean, when you put it like that, it's kind of hard. Don't use such big words like that. Use medium words tonight. Listen, whether you're the king of the jungle or a tiny chipmunk with busted eyeglasses, beauty is passion. And like I was saying, beauty attracts beauty. Just try to find someone with a passion for painting, music, eating fine fruits, or even roaming the forest frontier like you!"

"Traversing the forest frontier. Not roaming."

"You're missing the point. If you share your passion with the right gal, she'll see your beauty. Remember, most fellas fall in love with their eyes, but ladies fall in love with…?

"Their heart?"

"Bingo."

"Hey!" a voice hollered from behind us. "How about helping two ladies out, too?"

Two beautiful chipmunks waiting by the front door waved to us. One was wearing a bright yellow dress and matching yellow lipstick, while the other was in pink. Both had big, puffy hair, but the girl in pink had the most enchanting blue eyes.

"Quick, do I smell like cinnamon?" asked Chuck.

"You always smell like cinnamon. Why is that?" I replied.

"No time!" he said, walking back toward the bouncer.

Chuck handed him another roasted hazelnut.

"Those two foxy chipmunks right there are with us," he declared.

The two ladies quickly joined us.

"Oh my golly. Thank you, boys," said the chipmunk in pink. "My name is Jewel. This is my friend Sheila."

"Chuck Goldblum. Former AMF squadron, triathlon athlete, and certified translator. This is my pal, Rocky," said Chuck, walking Jewel toward the bar.

"Certified translator? In what language?" asked Sheila. Her high-pitched voice made me cringe.

"The language of adventure and love," replied Chuck, slicking his hair back from his forehead.

The gals laughed. I stood stiff, paws sweaty as I stared into Jewel's lovely eyes. Her entire being stood out like a middlemest flower, the rarest flower in the forest.

While Chuck and Jewel laughed and talked amongst themselves, I listened to Sheila rant about being friends with some famous singer, Elvis Pinecone. His hair. His accent. His clothes. On and on and on! I nodded my head out of respect, but wasn't paying much attention. I had eyes only for the gal in pink. She was pure beauty.

After an hour of small talk, Chuck made the next move.

"You two wanna shimmy outta here and get sorbet?" he asked.

"Maybe after one more crabapple? You never do what I want to do, Jewel!" cried Sheila.

"Excuse me? We always do what you want to do," said Jewel, arms folded. "Who's in the mood for lemon sorbet?"

"I like watermelon sorbet," said Sheila.

"So get watermelon sorbet. I prefer lemon sorbet with fresh honey. Oh my golly, I could eat an entire pot of honey right now! Shall we go?" asked Jewel.

Chuck burst out in laughter. "A pot of honey? How about a Honeypot?" he said, laughing even harder.

"A Honeypot? Aww, that's adorable. I'd love one," she replied.

Chuck nearly fell to floor in laughter.

"You don't talk much, do you?" Jewel inquired, walking awkwardly close to me.

"She doesn't know your name, Rocky!" announced Chuck, as he continued laughing.

Despite the awkward situation, I found myself lost once again in her eyes.

"Think you can beat me in a staring contest?" challenged Jewel, still nose to nose with me. "Don't blink."

"I won't blink. My name is Honeypot. Rockford T. Honeypot," I said, eyes filling with tears as I tried not to blink.

"What does the 'T' stand for?" she asked.

"Triumph."

"Really?"

"No. My mother loved to make tea."

"Snooze fest," Chuck said, yawning like a jaguar. "Rocky, forget what I said earlier. Go with some big words. Tell Jewel about photo-synthasicero."

"Get out!" she yelled, pushing me in the chest with excitement. "What do you know about photosynthesis?"

"Did you blink? I blinked after you pushed me, but let's have a do-over," I said, getting close to her again.

"You're nutty," she said, pushing me away once again. "Are you at Elderwood University? I haven't seen you around."

"No. I studied with the mindful monks and their Book of Light."

"Book of Light? We don't have that one." She giggled. "I'm

a first year, studying botany. Photosynthesis is a new discovery my professor theorized."

"There you go, Rocky! Don't be such a cane toad. Let's intellectualize!" interjected Chuck. I could tell he'd had one too many crabapples.

"Actually, it's not his theory, considering the monks wrote about the process many years ago," I explained.

"Her theory, but that's not the point. So, Rocky T. Honeypot," said Jewel, staring into my eyes, "what else is in that mind of yours behind your dashing charm and spicy good looks?"

I was stumped.

I had dashing charm and spicy good looks?

Me?

What were spicy good looks?

Chuck put his arm around Jewel, waiting for my response.

Confusion filled my thoughts. Panic was around the corner.

Say something. Anything!

"Definitely not chili peppers. They give me cramps."

How embarrassing.

"Ah, I love chili peppers!" Chuck interjected. "I wish they were in season."

"Actually, I've been hypothesizing something about that!" Jewel exclaimed. "If you could control the water intake and light in a sealed enclosure, the vegetation could be controlled in a way that would allow year-round growth! It's just a theory, and my professor thinks I'm toucan-cuckoo, but I think it could work."

"I've built them. They're called green-huts."

"Get out!" she shouted, pushing me in the chest again.

I fell to the ground, which was littered with enough germs to evoke further anxiety.

"You almost got me!" she continued. "My father runs the largest lumber company in Tropland. I'd know if you built one of those. Let's grab Sheila and get sorbet, okay? Come now, don't be such a house mouse."

"I just need to wash my paws first. The floor here is atrocious," I said.

"Wait, try this. Let me see your paws." Jewel reached into her purse for a small bottle of liquid. She squirted some onto my paws.

"What is this?" I mumbled.

"Paw sanitizer. It's all the rage now." She squirted some on her own paws. "Go on, wipe your paws together like soap. No water needed and it kills 99.9% of all bacteria, germs, and viruses."

"Get out!" I pushed her shoulder perhaps a touch too hard from the excitement.

"Keep it. I've got another," she offered, catching her balance.

"Break it up, germies. Don't go picking a fight on our first night. Let's swoop by Rocky's tree-hut first," Chuck said, grabbing Jewel's paw on the way out. "I left my scarf on his sofa."

"Chuck, you don't own a scarf," I whispered.

"Don't blow it. Let's just go hang out. I really like Jewel," he whispered back.

As we all walked out, I inspected the bottle of hand sanitizer. While my heart missed Sora, I'd never met a gal like Jewel before. I felt like this might be the start of a special friendship.

Unfortunately, less than an hour later, what had started as a wonderful night became a disaster. Upon arriving at my tree-hut, we found the entire left wall had been chewed away. The sight of an empty tree-hut made my stomach turn like a rotten banana.

"There's only one critter able to eat through wood with such precision," said Chuck.

"Termites!" I screamed.

"Is this your tree-hut?" Sheila whimpered. "You could use some furniture."

Everything was gone. I ran to my bedroom and dove under the bed where I hid my backpack. It was gone! All my furniture. All my stuff. My diamond. Gone!

I broke down in tears. Everything I had worked so hard for was taken. It was as if I had been cursed to live an unhappy life. Finally, the moment I felt a flake of happiness, it was ripped away from me like a leaf from its stem.

"The termite mob took our hut when I was a child!" I shouted in anger. "Now they continue to haunt me? I'll squish them all and wreak havoc on their tiny, ill-bred, infinitesimal faces!"

"Rocky, I'm all for revenge, but these are termites," Chuck warned. "I've seen their swamps. It's not pleasant."

"Stop lying! Nobody knows where they live."

"I do. We flew above their swamps a few times during AMF patrols. Dead trees, dead logs, and very humid."

"Then what are we waiting for? Let's go right now!"

"Hold it there, Rocky. They outnumber us like acorns versus oak trees. There's nothing much we can do except call the police. I'm sorry, Rocky," Chuck whispered.

As I wiped the tears from my eyes, Jewel stepped in front of me.

"I'm so sorry," she said. "My mother taught me that a hug is worth a million words."

Jewel put her arms around me. Her lemon oil perfume

soothed my nerves. I had lost everything that night, but for that brief moment, I found a Jewel worth more than all the unshelled diamonds in the sky.

CHAPTER 14
THE PROPOSAL

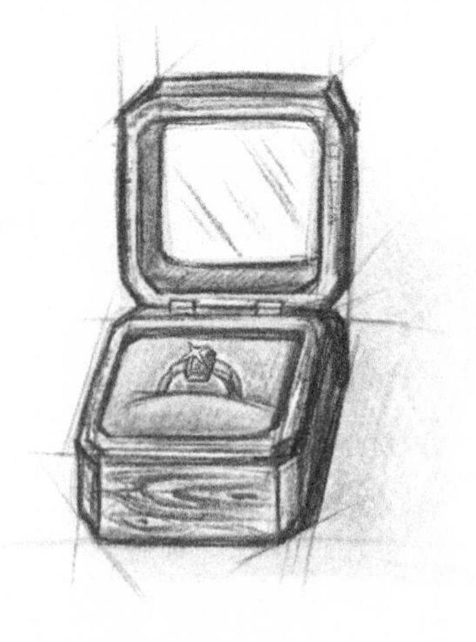

I had been staying at Chuck's tree-hut, considering mine was uninhabitable. Not only was everything gone, but the insect community and moss infestation invaded my living room like a decaying tree.

Despite losing everything, I was grateful for my loving friends who did their best to cheer me up. I'd only known Jewel for three months but felt I had known her for three lifetimes. We had become close friends during this period of time. Everything about her was precious to me—her cute, fuzzy ears, the way she nibbled on a crabapple, or how her face puckered with each spoonful of lemon sorbet. I even liked the way her cheeks puffed when talking about her relationship problems.

Chuck and Jewel started dating the evening we met. I was happy for Chuck who believed he had found his perfect match, though I wondered if they were right for each other. Jewel was always so calm, collected, and incredibly smart, while Chuck's intense personality was somewhat overbearing. Inevitably, their relationship was doomed. At least, so I thought.

"Chuck, do you think we should go with spinach or kale for the salad base?" I inquired, packing for a Saturday afternoon picnic. "Never mind, I think Jewel prefers spinach. Oh, and Sheila, too."

"Three hundred fifty-eight pushups… three hundred fifty-nine pushups… four hundred pushups!" exhaled Chuck forcefully with a laugh. Chuck's muscles had muscles that afternoon.

"Hey, Rocky. I've got the perfect plan. Let's drop by a fancy restaurant and order to go. I want this picnic to be perfect. Once we hike to the top of Wabua Falls, we'll have lunch, then go for a swim."

"Didn't your mother ever teach you not to eat before swimming?" I replied. "Swim first, then eat."

"Fine. After we eat, I have a special dessert for Jewel."

"Let me guess, lemon sorbet?"

"Even better, I'm going to ask her to marry me."

My heart cracked like a hazelnut.

"Chuck!" I exclaimed. "You just met her a few months ago. How can you ask her to marry you? What's her favorite vegetable? Do you… do you know her favorite fruit or whether she likes ginger in her mint tea? Does she prefer strawberries or raspberries? Lavender or chamomile? Think about it, Chuck. Do you even have a ring? Traditional protocol requires you ask her father for his blessing, you know." I couldn't breathe.

"Whoa! Calm down, Rocky. No, I don't know those things, but that's why I want to marry her—so I can learn everything about her! And I'd be honored if you would be my best chipper."

If my heart could have sunk deeper, it would have.

"Besides, I know she loves me," he continued. "I haven't felt this happy since my early days with the AMF."

Setting aside my feelings for Jewel, Chuck was my best friend. In my heart, I didn't believe she would accept his proposal. Chuck was going to be devastated! His bliss would be washed away by the waterfalls of Wabua. I couldn't let him suffer that kind of humiliation.

But what if I was wrong? What if Jewel said yes? I struggled to breathe.

Life was much simpler when my concerns were to stay hydrated and avoid fleas and ticks. Now, I was filling out police reports and dealing with lost love, conflict, drama, family regret, and more. My life had become the kind of tragedy I only read about in novels.

The time had come for our hike.

"As long as we stray a short distance from the river, we'll be clear of the snapping turtles," I spoke out.

"Snapping turtles wouldn't dare touch us, Rocky. Have you seen these biceps?" Chuck said, flexing through the sleeves of his jacket.

When we met up with Jewel, she was wearing a flowing pink floral dress. She looked beautiful.

Chuck wouldn't stop talking about his days in the AMF. Jewel appeared to be entertained by his stories, but every so often she would push her hair out of her eyes and gaze back at me.

Sheila, wearing an ugly yellow dress, kept tugging on my shirt, freaking out. Apparently, she didn't realize bees love yellow and was harassed throughout our hike.

When we finally reached the top of Wabua Falls, it was midafternoon. I pulled Chuck aside several times trying to dissuade him from proposing, but his stubbornness wouldn't have it.

In the distance, a large waterfall cascaded into two streams, dropping to where we planned to swim. A stunning rainbow flourished in the mist.

"What a perfect view!" Jewel shouted.

"You're a perfect view," Chuck said.

I couldn't watch.

Chuck grabbed Jewel's paw and knelt down on one knee.

Sheila chirped like a parakeet, clapping, giggling, and bouncing.

"Jewel, I've only known you a short time, but I love you," Chuck said softly.

"Chuck," she interrupted him, "what?"

"I said I love you!" exclaimed Chuck.

"Can we talk privately?" she whispered.

"Do you not love me? I… I thought you felt the same?"

"I think you're moving too fast right now." She took a few steps back. "Why don't we all have our picnic? What do you think, Rockford?"

"Are you in love with Rocky?" Chuck shouted.

"Excuse me?" She glared at him. "I think we all need to relax and enjoy our picnic."

"Spinach salad, anyone?" I interrupted, trying to ease the awkward situation.

"Oh, I love spinach salad," said Jewel as she tried to grab Chuck's paw. "Come on, let's eat."

"I'm so confused. Why don't you love me?" Chuck asked, pulling his paw away from her.

"I—I like you, Chuck. But sometimes, you're too intense. Please don't do this now."

"Do what? I'm too intense?" said Chuck, walking over to

the edge of the mountain. "Do you hear that, Rocky? I'm too intense!" He let out the loudest whistle I had ever heard.

A giant red-shouldered hawk darted toward Chuck from a distance.

"Hawk! Chuck, there's a hawk!" I yelled, grabbing Jewel to hide behind some bushes. Sheila followed. "Chuck! What are you doing?"

"What am I supposed to do, Rocky?" he yelled, holding back tears.

"To start, you can get over here! Remember your Tamias training. Move it!"

"You know what? Maybe this is how it was supposed to happen," he said, pacing back and forth on the edge of the cliff. "Maybe this was the fire I needed to return to my AMF squadron." He faced Jewel, vulnerability in full bloom. "If we waited, would you ever consider marrying me?"

"Chuck, PLEASE! Let's talk about this privately?" begged Jewel, remaining by my side.

"No, that's alright," he sighed, "I've embarrassed myself enough for the day."

"This is crazy! Get back here!" I pleaded.

"Crazy as a cashew! You will always be my brother, Rocky. Don't forget it! But I am and will always be *AMF*!"

He sprinted to the cliff and jumped off.

"CHUCK!" I yelled, running toward the edge.

The giant hawk dove down toward him.

A short moment later, the hawk shot up toward the sun with Chuck clutching its back feathers. I couldn't believe it. My best friend was now gone.

There are some events in life that take you by surprise. Sometimes they happen for a reason, other times, for reasons unknown. That was the last I heard from Chuck for a long,

long time. His leap of faith profoundly influenced my life. My best friend, who I had grown to love as a brother, had left me in the company of a gal who later became the love of my life.

Spoiler alert: it wasn't Sheila.

CHAPTER 15
THE NUTTY NUT

-Back to Green-Hut Market 39-

"Chuck just leapt off a cliff like that?" Theo asks, sitting on Randy's shoulder.

"Crazy as a cashew!" shouts Randy as he bounces Theo up in the air.

"I see we're becoming friends? Let's suppose a good quibble is good every once in a red moon." observes Rockford.

"Yeah, let's. We're golden," says Theo.

"Ooh, I'm a golden lion Tamarin!" replies Randy.

"Obviously." Theo shakes his head. "Yo-yo trick, anyone?"

Thunder cracks loudly in the distance. Raindrops trickle down the canopy toward the crowd. Luckily, everyone remains relatively dry from the dense leaves above the marketplace.

"Sure, let's see your new trick," says Rockford.

Theo stands closer to Rockford's leg, eyeing the lightning strikes above the canopy. "I'll… wait until the rain stops."

Rockford looks around at the animals huddled together.

"All of us come from different species and cultures. Yet here we are, crowded together under rainfall, telling stories as new friends. It's been a while since I've been in public like this. Thank you."

"Don't forget about the two hundred thousand critters watching online!" shouts Holly, turning her phone back toward her. "And don't worry internet friends, I've got a battery backup and a battery backup for that battery backup, so we're not going anywhere! You've officially gone viral, Rockford!"

"I've gone viral? As long as there's no fever," jokes Rockford, sharing a brief chuckle with Rosalina.

"Ooof. Going viral means you're popular, Great-granddad," whispers Theo.

"Oh, dear. It was a joke. At least someone found it funny," says Rockford, smirking at Rosalina. "Paw sanitizer, anyone?"

--

Three years had passed since Chuck made his leap of faith. Jewel was wrapping up her final year at Elderwood University, and the two of us were deeply in love. It took a few months to transition from being friends to sharing the same spoon for sweet lemon sorbet. I was all kinds of nuts about her! The way her cheek pouch puffed. The way she combed her long, tan hair in the morning and pulled it back into a chiptail. Jewel was the secret ingredient to my trail mix.

We rented a snug, one-bedroom tree-hut a bunny hop across campus. It wasn't the most elegant tree in the canopy, but we were together. Jewel and I enjoyed the simple things in life, unlike her parents, who enjoyed the regal life. They were one of the more affluent families in Tropland that lived like the mud couldn't stick to their paws. She told me stories about their surreal lifestyle; living with butlers, attending gala parties, and suing any critter who got in their way.

During this time, I worked in various restaurant kitchens as an assistant to the chef or a dishwasher. Nothing too memorable happened with these jobs. I kept my nose clean, working hard until I could afford an official fire license. Finally, I was able to build my own makeshift roasting oven at home. The shape was lopsided with two big cracks on the top, but it was all mine!

The delightful scent of roasted nuts often filled the tunnels near our grove. Elderwood campus is nearly four hectares, which is enormous. All the trees are connected to one another with bridge-like tunnels so the students and faculty can cross the campus more efficiently, even through bad weather. Our hut gave Jewel quick access to the botany department through the tunnels. It also provided yours truly with direct access to the library without getting wet, cold, hot, or sweaty.

The university librarian, an older tree squirrel, had a sweet tooth for my roasted cinnamon apple almonds. You needed student or faculty identification to enter the library, but in this case, a few roasted almonds in the return basket worked like a golden nugget.

When my whiskers weren't deep in adventure tales or books about modern law and agricultural economics, I perfected roasted pine nuts, pistachios, walnuts, and almonds. As a friendly gesture, I tossed some tasty nuts to students on my way to and from the library. Roasted nuts were not only delicious and satisfying, but enhanced productivity. Some of the students offered to pay me for them!

In an ironic twist of fate, I was following in the paw prints of generations before me. CC&C had been out of business for years, but hazelnuts were our family calling. Eve was still the Queen of the Jungle in terms of her roasting talents. She had new restaurants popping up all over Tropland. The students I had been meeting didn't have the time to wait in Eve's fancy restaurant lines, nor the money to buy roasted nuts in bulk. They purchased their food, like everyone else, at the local grocery-hut from a dismal selection of raw, flavorless nuts.

I packaged roasted nuts in small, individual to-go packets, perfect for the busy student or teacher. They came in three flavors: Terrific Thyme, Crunchy Cinnamon, and Radiant Rosemary. With a clever name that would make Eve proud as a peacock and a demand skyrocketing at Elderwood University, 'The Nutty Nut' quickly became a campus favorite. I roasted, toasted, and served up the finest nuts in the forest.

-Back to Green-Hut Market 39-

"Check this out, Great-granddad," says Theo, whirling his yo-yo around in circles. "This one is called the moon cycle!"

"Very good, Theo," Rockford replies, catching his breath as the crowd watches. "Where were we?"

"This is getting boring," Theo whispers, "I thought you said it was a short story?"

"I must have gotten carried away," Rockford sighs. "I thought you were enjoying our story time?"

"Great-granddad, 'story time'?"

"I love it," says Ann. Her dimples catch Theo's attention. "Was this when you proposed to Jewel?"

"After Jewel graduated, we had enough money to buy a larger tree-hut north of Elderwood," says Rockford. "I had planned to ask Jewel to be my wife that summer. However, I needed to get her father's approval first."

"May I sit with you while the story continues?" asks Ann, sitting next to Theo, who blushes.

CHAPTER 16
MAKING A SCENE

Everything was smooth as hazelnut butter until I had to ask Jewel's father for his blessing to marry his daughter. Her family was very traditional, and while I had only met her parents twice before, we weren't exactly peas in the same pod.

The first time I met her mother and father, we ate at The Lulo Club early in the evening. It was a ritzy restaurant run by deer mice, not too far from Elderwood. Of course, I wore my finest purple suit and trousers to compliment Jewel's flowing pink dress.

Upon our arrival, I was first introduced to Elizabeth Thicket, Jewel's mother. Elizabeth was dressed in a classy black and white dress with several ruby rings and other pieces of flashy jewelry.

"Mom!" Jewel shouted to catch her attention.

"Jewel, don't you have anything nicer to wear?" Elizabeth's smile looked shriveled and forced. "This is your father's favorite restaurant."

Jewel ignored her and pulled me forward by the paw. "Mother, meet my boyfriend Rockford."

"It's a pleasure to meet you, Mrs. Thicket." I bowed my head.

"What am I? The Queen of Tropland? I like this boy," she laughed.

"Is that my sweet Jewel?" boomed a scratchy, impressive voice. I turned, and there was Jewel's father, Jack Thicket. He wore a tuxedo as if it were his everyday clothing.

"Hi, Dad. Meet Rockford." Jewel nudged me in his direction.

"Hi," Jack said dismissively as he brushed right past my outstretched paw. "Tell me all about your first year after they serve breadsticks. I can't concentrate when I'm hungry." Jack then turned to acknowledge me, looking my purple suit up and down with an expression of distaste. "Nice to meet you, but our reservation is only for three. I'm sure you understand."

"Nonsense. I'll let them know we're here!" exclaimed Elizabeth.

"Dad," Jewel muttered, turning pink, "I told you Rockford was joining us this evening."

"You did?" demanded Jack. "Oh, well. Come on, Sparkles. Let's eat. Daddy's hungry."

"You're joking. I'm not going without Rockford!" Jewel said, taking a stance.

For a moment, Jack analyzed me again from head to toe. His stare felt like the judgement of a thousand lawyers.

"Sparkles, how many times do we need to discuss standards? We'll only be an hour or two. You don't mind, do you?"

"Umm… are you serious?" I asked.

"Father!" Jewel snapped.

"Your loss. Their breadsticks are tremendous. If you change your mind, we'll see you inside. Love you, Sparkles." And with that, Jack strode into the private dining area.

As we left, Jewel was so livid, steam was practically rising from her ears.

"That was… rude," I said.

"Welcome to the Thickets!" She kicked sod toward the restaurant. "Pretentious Cherrywood Jerk. And my mother does nothing about it. She's in her own world. I'm sorry, let's go somewhere else."

"No apology needed. You should have met my father. Minus the wealth, he was a fellow Cherrywood Jerk. Hmmm, more like a Walnut Wood Jerk!"

She smiled, kissing me on the cheek.

Her simple touch could turn negativity into utopia.

The second time I met her parents was after Jewel's third year at Elderwood. Her family threw a lovely get-together at The Bell Isle, another snooty restaurant an hour away from our home. Once again, I wore my best outfit to impress the Thickets.

"Sparkles! Come in, come in," said Jack, greeting us at the door. "Jack Thicket, nice to meet you."

He held out his paw, so I shook it. "Nice to see you again, sir."

"We've met?" He gazed at something else in the distance.

"When you rudely dismissed us for breadsticks!" sneered Jewel.

"Yes! Now I remember," Jack shouted as his eyes lit up. "Same guy, huh, Sparkles?"

At that moment, Jewel's younger brother, who was maybe five or six years old, came storming towards us.

"Is he the Nutty Nut?" the young chipmunk demanded.

"Yes. This is my boyfriend, Rockford. Rockford, meet Marshall, my brother."

"A pleasure to meet you," I said.

"Nutty Nut shot!" he shouted, punching me in the crotch, then ran off.

"Right in the gemstones!" Jack said, laughing.

"Marshall!" Jewel yelled. "I'm sorry. Here, drink this." She grabbed a glass from a waitress.

I chugged the black drink. It tasted sweet, salty, bitter, and sour, all at the same time.

"What the forest is this?" I sputtered.

The waiter, a duck in a white suit, handed me a napkin.

"A licorice puree with a blend of choice herbs," he said.

"Not my choice of herbs!" I replied, wiping my tongue with the napkin.

Jewel elbowed me in the arm.

"What?" Suddenly, my tongue felt completely numb. "Dosh my tom look odd to ye?" I slurred. My face swelled like a hedgehog's.

Someone called an ambulance and I was rushed to the hospital. Apparently, I'm allergic to licorice.

This third time, I had a diamond ring in my pocket and the stage was set. Elizabeth and Jack planned a lavish party at The Blue Butterfly for Jewel's big graduation. My plan was simple: ask for her father's permission, to which he'd likely say no, then propose anyway. At least I would be following traditional protocol.

It was a members-only private social club, the fanciest lounge I'd ever seen. It had a strict dress code, no jeans, no denim. Women had to wear dresses long enough to cover their knees, while men had to wear a mandatory blazer and tie. They even made us wear white covers over our paws, so no mud was ever tracked on their sapele wood floors.

This was an evening to remember, complete with extravagant cocktails such as mint gumdrops and watermelon martinis. Unfortunately, when I asked for a crabapple, several noses were pointed away in repulsion.

"We don't serve crabapples here," said the gopher bartender. "Perhaps you can find them at an establishment better suited to your kind."

"Don't worry about them, Rocky. These folks live in a parallel ecosystem," Jewel said quietly.

"But these are your parents and their friends. Wouldn't that be your ecosystem?"

"You're my ecosystem, you nut." She elbowed me in the belly. "Most of the paws in here haven't dug a hole their whole life. Have I mentioned how handsome you look in your red bow tie?"

We giggled.

The appetizers were nauseating. Both Jewel and I kept our distance at least three paces from each waiter to avoid the foul smells of caterpillar tartare, titan beetle pate, and leafhopper liver mousse.

If I were to eat just one of those, I'd likely get bacterial enteritis with an immediate onset of tummy troubles. Jewel's parents were so self-absorbed in their glitz and glamour, they didn't bother serving food their daughter would enjoy.

I was starting to understand why Jewel never liked talking about her parents, and why we only saw them once a year. Though I hadn't seen my parents in many years, I couldn't help but feel a seed of guilt for not tracking them down after all this time.

The Blue Butterfly lounge had a capybara and his jazz band playing throughout the evening. 'Let's be Frank' was the name of the band. You might think it clever if his name had been Frank, but it was Flipper.

Suddenly, Jack approached me, requesting I speak with him privately. We walked through a hallway lined with portraits of old, affluent animals.

"Braxton! Won't you join us?" he shouted down the hallway.

Braxton?

As we walked outside to the patio, several animals were mingling. We continued up a long spiral staircase to a more private setting.

"Rockford," Jack said in a mildly degrading tone. "You're a fine lad. My daughter appears to be very fond of you. But then again, a child is fond of roly-poly bugs and shiny leaves."

"Armadillidiidae," I corrected him.

"Say what now?

"Roly-polies are part of the Armadillidiidae family. Also referred to as a pill bug."

"I don't care. Did you know there are three kinds of chipmunks, according to the genus of our species? I like to call them the treasurer, the steward, and the housekeeper. Now, the treasurer, a chipmunk much like myself, seeks out riches and success beyond everyone else. I've built the largest lumber company in the entire forest. Look out there in the great Tropland Rainforest. What do you see in abundance?"

"Trees."

"Of course you see trees. I see money. Money is power. Therefore, when I look out onto our lands, I see power."

A tall, well-dressed chipmunk in a slim-fitting tuxedo came up the spiral staircase. His suave haircut, shiny teeth, and pompous sway irritated me like a bad skin rash.

"Ah, Braxton! Meet Rockford. Rockford, meet Braxton

McFudden III. Heir to the McFudden mustard seed empire of the South."

"How do you do, Rockford? Long time, friend," said the boy who gave me nightmares as a child.

I couldn't believe it. The fur on my neck stiffened with the memories of my childhood years.

"Braxton. Such a pleasure to see you," I snarled.

His grip was overcompensating in strength. Luckily, digging out weeds and sod with the monks over the years gave me an advantage. I squeezed his paw with the force of ten thousand chipmunks. He may have been smiling for Jack, but he felt my mighty grip.

"I'm not the same chipmunk I was years ago, old friend," I said, squirting paw sanitizer to clean my paws from his muck.

"I'm giving young Rockford here a valuable life lesson. Won't you join us?" Jack continued. "Braxton here is also part of the treasurers in Tropland—a fine young chipmunk who dated my Jewel before leaving for Kale graduate school."

"Excuse me? You two dated?" I asked.

"Jewel and I were tight as sap on a leaf," said Braxton with a smirk.

I could crush a dozen hazelnuts with my jaw in that moment. I was calm on the outside, but fuming with rage on the inside.

"That's why we're all here tonight: to reconnect with old friends and celebrate the future of Tropland," Braxton said with his picture-perfect jaw line. "Rockford and I used to know each other as children. In fact, I used to call him 'Furpee boy.'"

"Furpee boy? How original!" Jack chuckled. "Like I was saying, following the treasurer, we have the steward. Jewel told me a bit about how you worked for Eve Pippens, the celebrated chef, pioneer of the recent roasting craze. Now, there's a prime example of a successful steward. In Eve's case, the kitchen is her domain!"

"Where most ladies do their best!" Braxton interrupted.

The two dimwits shared a good laugh.

I shook my head in disgust.

"Quality joke, Braxton!" Jack chortled. "A steward is in command of the household and makes an honest living with their craft. Stewards cannot afford a lavish life of luxury, but are certainly comfortable."

Jack looked at me with an intense gaze. "Finally, we have the housekeeper," he continued. "They may or may not work for a living and more than likely scrape for a chance at greatness. They never attain anything more than the fantasy of their hopes and dreams. There's nothing wrong with being a housekeeper. They make decent company, maintain a degree of cleanliness, and are the backbone of our species as the working class of Tropland."

"Though in some areas, they can use more cleanliness, if you ask me," Braxton chimed in.

They chuckled like a pair of Amazon milk frogs.

"Forgive me if I'm too brash in presenting all this information, considering the lack of communication we've had in the past," said Jack, placing a cigar in his mouth.

"Allow me." Braxton lit the cigar with a match.

"Thank you, son." Turning back to me, Jack continued, "Rockford, you're the housekeeper of our species, and certainly do not belong with a treasurer like my precious Jewel. After all, even her name is beyond your reach."

The smoke from Jack's cigar was disgusting.

"Look around. This life is not yours to live," he continued. "The elegance. The wealth. The prestige. I've chartered a transport goose for my family to travel to Arrow Oaks next week. We have a third home there, close to where Jewel can get her graduate degree. Maybe even marry someone with a bright future ahead of him. Say, in the mustard business?"

Jack and Braxton embraced yet again, chuckling.

The chip-mance between these two was revolting.

"As her father, do me a kindness and wish Jewel the best of luck this evening. Say your goodbyes early before this becomes too emotional and causes a scene. Elizabeth hates scenes. Let's be civil about the matter."

I couldn't believe this nutcracker!

Of all the famous writers who wrote about tragedy and anger, the poem from Ka came to my mind.

Each day a journey.

A battle of blood or heart.

To live is to love.

This was a battle for love. One that I refused to lose.

"You know nothing about me!" I said with my head up and chest out. "You know nothing of the experiences and the journeys I've traversed to be here today. You think you've earned the right to speak down to me like that because you 'own' Tropland?"

"He speaks down to you because you're short," snickered Braxton.

"I may not be a so-called treasurer, but I've got the greatest currency in the forest: LOVE. If you think you can make decisions on who Jewel loves, you are way out of touch with the ecosystem."

"I said I don't want to cause a scene. Let me stop you right there," Jack snarled.

"With all due respect, I'm talking now." I put my hind paw down. "A few years ago, your words would have hurt me as much as the verbal scars I carry from my father or the rotten memories of Braxton's childish monkeyshines. I'm not the same chipmunk I used to be. Since meeting Jewel, we've become happier than a flowering fig tree."

"Now listen here, Furpee boy!" Braxton stepped forward angrily, breaking a wooden floorboard.

"Father! Braxton! Rockford!" shouted Jewel, climbing up the spiral staircase.

"Jewel, we were just talking about you. How've you been? You look exotic in that dress," said Braxton.

"Cut it, Braxton," Jewel snapped, "we heard every word you boys said."

Braxton and Jack looked down to find Elizabeth surrounded by guests staring back up in shame.

"How dare you make decisions about my future and who I choose to love," Jewel continued. "And Braxton, we never dated! You two live in a fantasy!"

"Jewel! Listen to me," said Jack. "I know what's best for you. I don't want you throwing your life away when I've worked so hard for your future."

"He is your father, Jewel. Can we talk for a moment?" said Braxton.

"I said cut it, Braxton! I haven't liked you since we met in the fourth grade, and nothing's changed. I'm so embarrassed by your words, Father. Rockford is a sweet chipmunk whom I love with every whisker. Thank you for this unforgettable evening. We're leaving!"

Jewel grabbed my paw and pulled me toward the staircase. I nearly twisted my ankle knocking over a large pot of azaleas which crashed onto the broken floor board. Instantaneously

SMACK!

The other end of the wooden slat snapped upward between Braxton's legs, hitting him square in the tassel berries.

Elizabeth gave us each a hug and a kiss as we walked back inside.

"Congratulations on graduating, darling. Don't listen to him, Rockford," she said. "He'll hear it from me later. See you two lovebirds soon!"

We ran down the long hallway toward the live music. I felt it in my bones that this was my moment. I grabbed the microphone from the jazz singer entertaining the crowd.

"Jewel. My darling Jewel." My voice echoed throughout the entire restaurant.

Everyone turned their heads my way.

"Oh my golly, Rocky. What are you doing?" Jewel whispered.

"Making a scene. I've loved you from day one and will continue loving you as long as the sun shines bright and the moon lights the night."

"Jewel!" shouted Jack, running toward us with Braxton and Elizabeth by his side.

Elizabeth elbowed him in the belly.

"You will NOT ruin this for our daughter. Be happy, you grouch," she demanded.

I knelt on one knee, held Jewel's beautiful paw, and took out the ring from my inside jacket pocket.

"You are my one and only Sunpot. My one and only Moonpot. Will you marry me and be my one and only Honeypot?"

"Yes! Absolutely, yes! A thousand yesses," she cried, tears running down her puffy cheeks.

"Right on, brother, right on. Let's get this music flowin'!" shouted Flipper. We stayed several hours more, dancing the night away.

CHAPTER 17
PLANTING ROOTS

Several months before our wedding, Jewel and I traveled to Rica Canyon in search of my family. The whole area had burned down from an earlier forest fire. Upon our arrival, a monkey construction worker informed us that all residents had migrated east. We searched the treetops, branches, and the eastern forest communities for two months, yet came up short. It was time to head home and move forward with our big day.

We were married in a private treetop lounge that had it all: decadent orange hanging lights, multi-colored dragonflies at every branch, valet nail buffing, a mixture of stomach-turning appetizers, and a fourteen-course meal. Although Jack never apologized for his past behavior, he and Elizabeth were very kind the whole evening. They paid for the entire celebration and bought Jewel her dream wedding dress with slivers of pink rosebuds intertwined on the sleeves and skirt.

Most of the tree was filled with Jewel's family and their

friends, many of whom Jewel nor I had ever met. Despite the multiple strangers attending our big day, there were a few friendly whiskers that showed up on my behalf! Eve and her new squirrel boyfriend arrived early with a basket of roasted goodies. Farley and his new muskrat friend, along with the Brentwood Brothers, Simon and Leo, joined us in our celebration. I hadn't seen the whole gang since we split from the Evening Musk years ago.

"Congratulations, ya nutty nut! You sure did fill out!" Eve said. "You've come a long way from knocking yourself out on the ice. Remember that? Jewel, be careful with this one. He's a fragile super-genius."

"Congrats, Rhubarb! I'm proud of ya," Farley boasted as he gave us a big squeeze.

"Thank you. Where did you go, big guy?" I joked.

"Lost a tree-load of weight an' started yoga!" He took his companion's paw gently. "All thanks to Carlos."

"You're a miracle worker, Carlos!" Simon joked.

"He works miracles!" blurted Leo, giving Simon a fist bump.

"You're far too kind," said Carlos, glancing at Farley with an endearing gaze. "While I appreciate the credit, the only miracle here was finding true love."

I was excited to see my old friends, especially grumpy Farley being so happy and festive with Carlos. After all, it was Carlos who later told me, 'Love is like a berry. Countless varieties. Sometimes sour. But when you find a good one, life sure is sweet.'"

It was a good thing our wedding was so memorable, since there was no time for a honeymoon. Jewel was offered an amazing job opportunity leading the Innovations Department at Elderwood University's state-of-the-art botany lab while completing her last year of graduate school.

Jewel's new job required working long hours throughout the day, so I kept myself busy reading at the library and roasting the finest nuts on campus. Known as 'The Nutty Nut,' my reputation as a gourmet roaster spread throughout the campus tunnels. I sold out every batch of my roasted treats by the time I reached the library.

From accounting to zoology, I couldn't stop reading. Everyone must have thought the infamous Nutty Nut was a professor, considering the number of hours spent in that library. On numerous occasions, I noticed a tall, thin, red-haired squirrel sitting in a corner with a stack of books as high as the library's massive computer, housed in a wooden frame.

"Pardon me," I asked one day. "I noticed you only have programming books. Do you care for the arts, botany, or philosophy?"

"Not really. I find comfort in programming," he replied.

"I'd love to learn programming. Is it difficult?"

"Yes."

"Think I could learn it?"

"How would I know? I don't know you."

"I'm the Nutty Nut. You may have heard of me?"

I realized this small talk was going nowhere. He wanted nothing to do with me. "The Nutty Nut? Packages of nuts?" I gave him a packet. "Rockford T. Honeypot. Nice to meet you."

"Billy Fence." He slowly looked up toward me, making eye contact for the first time. "Did you say Rockford? You know, there's a classic book series called The Adventures of Captain James T. Rockford."

"Classic? The most celebrated book series of my entire collection."

"Be bold and blossom," he said.

"To all the animal kingdom—may we never find a forest so extinct, waters so cold, bellies so empty that we can't fill them with love and joy," we exclaimed in our loudest library voices.

"Tropland's lack for developing hardware restricts our software progression. Programming is difficult but 'learn to deal with the bees if you want to enjoy the honey'," he said, snorting with laughter.

From that day forth, even though I didn't understand him half the time, we were pals. It turned out Billy was a professor of engineering and programming at the university. He was only a few years older than me, but looked old enough to be my father. His oversized pea-green sweater, beige shorts, and rectangular eyeglasses made him stand out from the crowd.

At a time when most of the forest was still using typewriters, Elderwood was one of the only universities with computers and a programming interest. He had been working on new computer software for years. Billy spoke passionately about his vision of the future where computers wouldn't be the size of gorillas, they'd be smaller than a jackfruit. He was certain they'd be in every school, company, and tree-hut across the forest.

Later that winter, the vision of 'my future' came earlier than I anticipated. My conversations with Billy changed from discussing auxiliary storage units to how to change diapers. Jewel shared the sensational news that I was going to be a father!

Typically, chipmunks have a litter of up to nine babies, but later that spring, Jewel had just one baby girl. She was the apple of our eyes, so you can guess what we named her.

Apple Honeypot looked just like her mother, with aqua-blue eyes and cheeks my mother would be proud to pinch. She was our little peanut. When she opened those eyes and looked at me for the first time, I felt her staring into the very fiber of my being. I felt the energy of the forest ecosystem, from the treetops to the sub-floor. Such a surreal feeling gave me warmth and comfort more than any roasted hazelnut. Side by side with my beloved Jewel, I was very happy with my life.

Around the same time, we were graced with the best neighbors in the forest! Billy, his lovely wife, Maude, and their two daughters moved next door to us.

As much as I loved hanging out with our new neighbors, I spent most of the time with Jewel, looking after our sweet Apple.

We never argued.

Well, maybe once or twice.

"Rocky?" Jewel yelled, looking around the hut.

"In here, lovepot!" I replied, wrapping Apple in her favorite blue blanket.

Jewel came in, looking a bit flustered.

"Look at you two. I wish I had our camera to take a picture, but it's probably next to my keys and everything else I can't find in this hut."

"Did you check the table by the door? I saw the camera earlier."

"I was talking about the keys. Where did you put the keys?"

"Did you check the ring hook near the door?"

"Of course. I'm so late," she said, her voice growing louder.

"Oh dear! Is your tropane alkaloid presentation today? I thought it was tomorrow!"

"It's today, Rocky. I don't know where anything is and I'm late and I'm nervous!"

"Let's not raise our voices. Apple is sleeping. Did you pack your samples?"

"What good is a lecture on toxic plants without samples? You're not helping!"

"Let's calm down. Focus on your breath," I said gently.

"I don't need any of your Mount Ego wisdom right now. Will you be home this evening?"

"I was planning on visiting Billy later with—"

"Great! So I don't need keys. See you in a few hours. Kisses to my beautiful Honeypots!"

After Jewel left, Apple wouldn't stop crying. I tried everything in my power to make her stop.

Let's try a nap, sweet Apple?

Cry.

Let's try cleaning your diaper, sweet Apple?

Cry.

Let's burp, sweet Apple?

Cry.

Blue blanket?

Cry.

Too hot? Let's take this blanket off.

Cry.

Too cold? Let's put this blanket back on.

Back inside.

Still crying.

How about some roasted hazelnuts?

A touch of this, a pinch of that. Fresh, roasted hazelnuts coming right up!

Parenting is hard!

The crying escalated to a full-blown temper tantrum.

At least my roasted cinnamon and blackberry hazelnuts were cooling down. I was ready to turn her gloomy cries into a happy surprise.

"Open wide, baby girl," I said, trying to give her a freshly roasted hazelnut.

She refused, smacking the hazelnut across the room.

"One more try. These were made just for you with love. Watch Daddy eat them. Yummy! In fact, I'll eat two. Nom, nom, nom!"

Weird aftertaste, I thought to myself as I chewed. My mouth felt dry as well. And why was the room spinning?

"Let's Apple," I mumbled. "Come room on sit couch with Daddy?"

I swiped the nuts into the trash as I stumbled for the couch. As soon as I made it there, everything went dark.

"Wake up! It's me, Billy! Billy Fence!" I could hear a voice shouting from above me.

I could feel his warm, clammy paws forcing what tasted like burnt chalk into my mouth.

"Rockford. Can you hear me? The ambulance is on its way. I found charcoal left from burnt coconut husks in your oven pit. I need you to swallow some. You must have eaten something poisonous."

"Apple?" I whispered, spitting the charcoal out.

"Apple is safe. Eat some charcoal, please. It'll help soak up the poison."

A week later, I returned from the hospital. I wasn't exactly back to normal, but I was feeling better. Jewel wouldn't leave my side. This time, she was the one crying nonstop! In her rush, she'd left a nightshade berry in the kitchen—a very poisonous berry which was part of her lecture that evening.

This was the first time Billy made a significant impact on my life. He came over to share a new book and found me passed out in the kitchen. His quick thinking and perfect timing saved my life.

For the record: I didn't think I could dislike anything more than germs or termites, but nightshade berries were now top on my list of things to avoid.

CHAPTER 18
DAWN OF MULBERRY

It took several months to recover from the nightshade berry debacle. Jewel took a leave of absence from work and school to take care of me and Apple. During my recovery, I felt sick to my stomach with anything I bit, chewed, or swallowed. At first, I was grouchy and irritable like my bowels. The rumbling in my belly was matched by the roar of desire to find my strength. With each sunrise, I chose to be a little more bold and blossom like the flowering purple orchids in the canopy. Come rain or shine, this lovely cluster of flowers never complained, never doubted themselves, and never looked back in time with regret. They flourished with inspiring strength and beauty.

Apple and I spent time solving math puzzles, while Jewel and I continued our endless discussions about the future of green-huts. Once my energy fully returned, I encouraged Jewel to continue her pursuit of success. She quickly become a superstar in the botany field, giving lectures across the forest on behalf of Elderwood University.

Billy, who worked harder than a toothless pocket gopher in a pile of hickory nuts, found the time to come visit for daily chats on my rooftop. He was very stressed from balancing family, teaching, and long hours of computer work. This gracious red squirrel had saved my life. I didn't mind listening to him blow off steam, plus, nothing stopped Apple's midafternoon whimpers more effectively than Billy's programming babble.

"Programming shares similarities with Kern," I said, flipping through one of Billy's thick books. "It reminds me of the vast, underground networks created by mushrooms."

"You said I'm the one who babbles?" replied Billy. "I've never heard of Kern. Explain."

"An ancient language I learned from my time with the mindful monks. Long story."

"I've got time."

I taught Billy the Kern basics, which in turn provided new insights to his work. Even Apple picked up on the lingo!

"Dos," Apple said in her cute, high pitched voice. "Dos! Dos! Dos!"

My baby's first word was in a language known to only six other animals in the forest! "Dos" means connection in Kern.

We had joked that if Kern was the missing link he needed to complete his software, Billy would have to name the company after Apple. He gave it some thought, but decided to name his company Mulberry, Captain James T.'s favorite fruit of the forest.

Jewel cancelled most of her lectures over the coming months once we got even more great news. She was pregnant once again!

I cleaned every inch of the tree-hut, the outdoor branches, the rooftops, and even part of the tree trunk. Most importantly,

I splurged on premium mosquito nets atop every bed and crib to ensure our hut was a peaceful palace for the new baby Honeypots—three more girls and one boy!

Violet, Olive, Lily, and… Clarence.

Just kidding!

Do you really think I'd name my firstborn son Clarence?

In book four of 'The Adventures of Captain James T. Rockford,' he is sent to investigate a mysterious distress call from the canopy of the Great Amazon. Upon the Captain's arrival, a stubborn chipmunk named Chester saves his life from a pack of deadly nocturnal bats. Chester helps Captain James T. rescue the kidnapped queen, who later has them knighted for their heroism. Captain James T. Rockford and his new best friend, Commander Chester, had many more adventures together throughout their lives.

Weighing in at a solid five grams was my son, Chester Honeypot.

My heart was overflowing with love, yet I still felt sorrow for Billy and Maude. They were like beautiful acorns stuck in a hard place. Billy had invested everything into his company and could barely afford food even as he worked endless hours.

Billy was not going to suffer on my watch! Sales of The Nutty Nut combo packs were on the rise, so we could afford to buy double groceries for as long as it took until Billy was able to launch his company properly.

To bring back that much food was difficult using the standard transport goose. Two times a week for eight months I'd follow Chuck's protocol: climb to the tallest tree, find myself a hawk, and travel to various farms in order to purchase fruits, veggies, nuts, grains, and seeds for both of our families. I not only proved to myself that I was capable of travelling solo on a hawk, but was also able to procure enough food for the

Honeypots and the Fences to eat until all our bellies were full.

The Fence family was grateful beyond fur. To show his appreciation, Billy asked to join me one morning.

"In the spirit of Captain Rockford T, I'm ready to hawk glide!" Billy howled with enthusiasm before we began proper protocol.

It wasn't long before we were soaring through the chilled air on the back of a large black hawk! Within twenty minutes, Billy lost his sweater and glasses while nearly freezing like an icicle.

"How do you make it stop?" he shrieked, holding onto the hawk's feathers for dear life.

"Put your finger in his ear! Like this!" I yelled.

As we descended, he yanked out a feather by mistake.

SQUAWK!

The young hawk spun out of control, bumping against the canopy branches. Leaves were slapping us around until we flew off the hawk into a stinky, vile swamp.

"Gross! I think I swallowed SWAMP water!" I cried out. "Swim to that tree, its branches are in the sun!"

When I turned my head, Billy was nowhere in sight.

This can't be good.

"BILLY!" I yelled.

No response.

I dove underwater several times with no luck until a few bubbles in the distance caught my attention. The deep, milky brown filth was no easy task to navigate. With a deep breath, I plunged through the muck until I bumped into Billy's arm, bringing him back up to the surface. He coughed up water while I paddled us toward the tree to safety.

"What… what was I thinking?" cried Billy, coughing up more water. "I'll stick with reading the stories, not participating in them!"

"Are you alright?" I asked, wiping filth from every part of my body.

"Yes, I believe all my parts are functioning," he replied, lying on the branch from exhaustion. "I saved your life, you saved mine," Billy mused. "What an interesting friendship we have. Thank you."

"You're welcome," I said, taking off my shirt. "We'll need to rinse this rotten filth from our clothes as quickly as possible. There's some clean rainwater in the leaves above."

We felt rather ridiculous that afternoon; stranded in our underwear like wandering potoo birds. I was uncomfortable in my purple briefs, but when I saw Billy's polka-dotted green briefs, I couldn't stop laughing.

"I'm a creature of habit," he said, lying in the sun. "Maude bought me twelve pairs when we were married. Choosing my briefs each morning is one less decision I have to make on a daily basis."

"I didn't say anything." I smirked, doing my best to stop laughing.

"Rockford, while I was motionless in the swamp, mere seconds from entering the great beyond, thoughts rushed to my head. Do you toss all the charcoal in the trash when you're done roasting?"

"That's what popped into your head?"

"Yes."

"Well, yeah. I throw it out."

"My great-great-grandmother used to make us charcoal biscuits as children when we were bloated from too many walnuts. Charcoal is helpful for not only accidental poisoning, but works wonders for tummy troubles. Don't throw it out."

"Good to know," I mused.

He sat up to stretch. "Also, we should have one central marketplace instead of having specialized grocery-huts scattered across the forest. It would be extremely efficient and less dangerous."

"That's a nifty—"

"If I used a piece of cedarwood under my chair, it would stop making noises," he interrupted with a rush of thoughts. "I'd like to bake a cake for Maude's birthday next week. A chameleon's tail has the same geometric spiral as a seashell. The foundation of my programming is off by a fraction of a decimal. Can you believe after all this time, the end result is a mere fraction?"

A moment of silence.

Finally, Billy whooped. "Once I make the fix, the software will be complete. I'm going to take a brief nap now. Please wake me in two hours."

Before I could reply, he was fast asleep.

Several hours had passed. Though our clothes had been cleaned, they were still too wet to wear.

"Rockford," he said, squeezing the water from his trousers. "I suppose now is a good time to tell you something important to me. I've gone ahead and carved out twenty-five percent of Mulberry in your name. Non-negotiable."

I'd been lazily watching a baboon try to scratch his back, but that got my attention. "What?"

"My company. Mulberry. A quarter ownership will be in your name."

"I'm flattered, but you know my paws are full with The Nutty Nut. I don't have the time nor judgement to be that involved."

"No, no, no. You don't have to work. It's a gift. My way of thanking you for your dear friendship, and for saving my life."

"You don't have to thank me. You're my friend," I said, holding my amethyst stone up toward the sunlight. A purple light shone across the tree onto a few wild pond-apples. "Oh! Wanna split an apple?"

"Yes, thanks," he said as I climbed toward the apples. "You know how each tree in the forest is in a constant cycle of absorbing carbon and producing oxygen?" Billy continued, going on one of his quick talking rants. "This swamp stinks with dense air while the understory is full of life. What if all the trees were connected in a network? Everyone would have access to all the oxygen."

"Here you go, half an apple," I said, breaking the green apple into two pieces. "What about the oxygen?"

"Never mind the oxygen. It was a metaphor. Owning a fourth of Mulberry doesn't require work. You'll be what's known as a silent partner. This is a token of gratitude for all your support."

"In that case, thank you very much. I appreciate it." I made two cups from a leaf and filled them with water. "Let's raise our cups to health, happiness, and a chance to change the forest. Cheers to both ears!"

We clinked our leaves together. "To all the animal kingdom!" we shouted in unison, "May we never find a forest so extinct, waters so cold, or bellies so empty that we can't fill them with love and joy!"

As you all know, Billy's small Mulberry seedling grew to be one of the biggest trees in Tropland. Within a year, Billy and his family moved to a larger tree-hut on the opposite side of Elderwood, where he opened a fancy corporate office. A year later, purchases for computers across Tropland were growing faster than palm trees. Wouldn't you know it, Mulberry software was the primary software for every single one! The very next year after that, Mulberry grew into the largest forest-wide technology corporation publicly traded on Tropland's stock market. Billy was even named Animal of the Year by 'Animal' magazine!

By the time Apple was five years old, Billy Fence had become Tropland's youngest billionaire.

-Back to Green-Hut Market 39-

"If Billy Fence became a billionaire, that made you a millionaire, right?" asks a prairie dog from the crowd.

Rosalina taps the youngster on the nose. "Is everything about money?"

"Yep," boasts the prairie dog.

"Don't count others' money," Rockford admonishes. "It's a bad habit."

Ann twirls Theo's yo-yo nearby, batting her eyelashes. "You dropped this. Mind if I play with it for a little while?"

Theo tenses up, standing speechless for a few seconds before hiding behind Rockford.

"How cute are they?" Rosalina whispers.

"Oh, to be young again," Rockford whispers back.

Holly flies in closer to the group. "Five hundred thousand viewers and climbing! Hashtag Rockford Origin Story is still the number one Whisker sticker!"

The crowd erupts in applause.

"Oh, ripe nectarines! How exciting," Rockford says, fixing his bowtie. "One moment I'm paying rent for a small, two-bedroom tree-hut, the next I have enough money to buy an entire grove of trees. My life had changed more drastically than the seasons, yet this was the dawn of an extraordinary new adventure.

CHAPTER 19
THE BUSINESS KNACK

Animal: Magazine Publication #251
Snippet from the article, "Billy Fence: Animal of the Year"
Written by Carol Cappella

"Billy Fence, a red-haired squirrel, is the most talked about animal of our generation. The Mulberry Founder and President is being hailed as the pioneer of the computing age and praised as a modern-day tycoon. Along with his board of directors and prosperous Mulberry stock shareholders, the company's river of wealth flows across the forest. How will this new technology evolve? What's next for Tropland? Whatever the answer, Billy Fence and his Mulberry experts are steering this technological tree upward."

KNOCK. KNOCK. KNOCK

"Rocky! Can you get the door?" shouted Jewel from the other room.

Wearing my fancy new purple robe and purple slippers, I opened the front door to find three young raccoons in dark maroon suits.

"Hello, Rockford Honeypot," the shortest raccoon spoke up. "We're here on behalf of the Call of Catchuba. Have you read any of our teachings?"

They each held a small book close to their hearts.

"No, I haven't. Do I know you boys?"

"No, Rockford Honeypot. No, you do not. We read about you and your latest achievement with Mulberry. We were hoping to discuss the Call of Catchuba with you in hopes of securing a generous donation to our cause. We are building a new hut for our members south of Elderwood. May we come in?"

"I've never heard of the Call of Catchuba. What is it about?"

"Not interested! Thank you for stopping over." Jewel appeared next to me and closed the door. "Darling, please don't egg on solicitors. All they want is your money."

"They seemed like nice critters..."

"Trust me, they will shine your bowtie six ways to Sunday for a donation. They used to come to our house all the time asking my father for money until he brought in Tiberius to guard the gates."

I had saved money from Nutty Nut sales, but when Mulberry became the hottest stock on the market, my bank account went through the treetops! It was time to move to a taller tree where we purchased a half acre of land for extra privacy from solicitors.

Ever since I stayed in Eve's rental-hut, I'd fantasized about living within the luxury of sapele wood. A large crew of beavers spent four months building our new tree-hut which spanned three branches. Jewel was a master at interior design, adding splashes of colorful art and stylish modern furniture. Personally, my style of interior design focused on functionality.

We employed a tough group of woodpeckers to carve a safety-hut deep in the base of our tree using reinforced iron bark, the hardest wood in the forest. The best part? A manual elevator was fastened to the tree-trunk, so we could be lowered to the safety-hut with ease.

Brilliant!

Now that we were safe and secure from germs and disasters, I had fun buying gifts for the whole family. The kids were easy to shop for, but Jewel's present required more thought. Jewel had grown up with extravagant gifts, so I had to buy her something special, something unique.

Something with lemons!

When we went to restaurants, she always ordered lemon water. When we cleaned our home, she used lemon oil. I decided to buy Jewel every lemon product I could find! Delivered in a large basket in the shape of a lemon was lemonade. Lemon sorbet. Lemon energy bars. Lemon cupcakes. Lemon cookies. Lemon pudding. Preserved lemons. Lemon curd (not my favorite). Lemon pie. Lemon candles. Lemon perfume. Lemon disinfectants. Lemon soap. A necklace with a gold lemon pendant. Rose gold earrings shaped like lemons. My personal favorite, a lemon quartz ring, the gemstone of the month for my April-born wife.

Over the next eighteen months, we were busy in our new hut and happy raising our scurry of little fluff tails. Young Apple, with her hair tied in a chip-tail, wearing her new circular eyeglasses and striped blue dress, could speak half a dozen languages by the age of seven. We explained to her that most species across Tropland spoke the same language, but her drive to learn couldn't be stopped. She soaked up knowledge like moss on a frosty spring morning.

Once our family settled into the groove of success, Jewel

and I moved forward with our passion project. With the discounts her father gave us on lumber, we built the green-huts of our dreams. From functionality and style to custom frames, doors, and hardware, we spared no expense. After all, we now had the land, the resources, and the knowledge.

Imagine the pleasure we got from seeing our first two green-huts fully completed within ten months. They were enormous! One was filled with a wide variety of fruits including five different types of lemons, while the other had all our favorite vegetables. We had planted over a hundred different foods to be harvested in six months or less.

The one thing missing was my mother. If only I could show her that I'd become the Captain Rockford T. Honeypot we both had imagined.

Jewel knew the difficulties I'd had in locating my family over the years. Her warmth and kindness in the pursuit of finding my family was admirable. We agreed that I'd go out for one more month in search of them once again.

The next week, my bag was packed with the essentials. I gave a gentle goodbye kiss to Apple, Violet, Olive, Lily, and Chester, then a not-so-gentle goodbye kiss to Jewel. I loved kissing that face!

"I'll see you soon, my love. Be safe." She kissed my cheeks.

"'Safe' is my middle name." I puffed my chest out.

"No, it's not," Apple interrupted. "It's Tea. The second most consumed beverage in Tropland."

"When did you get so smart?" I said, kneeling down to her cute, pointy whiskers.

"I've always been smart," she replied, adjusting her circular eyeglasses. "I assumed you already knew this about me, Daddy?"

KNOCK. KNOCK. KNOCK.

she truly adored Nutty Nut almonds. At first, Jewel and I thought it was simply professional courtesy that she came over daily to review the lawsuit. The kids loved to watch her fit eight roasted almonds in her mouth at once! After a few weeks, I had to increase my almond roast batch just to accommodate her visits.

One evening, Sue-Ann came over to deliver good news. Apple was learning another exotic foreign language, Chester was wrapping his orange shirt around his head, while the rest of the kids were taking a nap.

"These almonds are delicious as always, Chef Honeypot," she said. "After all these months of back and forth, my favorite moments were seeing you with your gorgeous family and sampling your roasted almonds."

"Thank you. Did you know almonds are part of the peach family?" I asked.

"Yes, of course. I'm an almond enthusiast."

"Apricots are part of the peach family, too!" Apple yelled from the other room.

"Any news on our lawsuit?" asked Jewel.

"Cut straight to the chase." Sue-Ann nodded approvingly. "I've always liked that about you, Jewel. I'm here today to share two lovely pieces of information. First, congratulations, the lawsuit is officially over!"

We jumped for joy, embracing each other, though I knocked over some utensils and kitchenware with my tail by accident.

"A lawsuit of this manner could have lasted longer than the Kurinji plant takes to blossom," Sue-Ann continued. "Braxton finally realized the costs were too severe to continue. They had no legal basis, and it is therefore now over!"

"Thank you for your healthy work ethic, Sue-Ann!" I said.

"At first, I was afraid of their chipmunk legal team. Not anymore!"

"Rockford?" Jewel interrupted. "Are you implying that you're impressed because she's a squirrel going against chipmunks?"

"What? No. I'm by no means an animalist. I love all species, from chipmunks to attractive squirrels like Sue-Ann."

"Attractive?" Jewel elbowed me in the chest.

"I mean beautiful, in a friendly way. Oh dear."

"Rockford?" Jewel elbowed me again.

"Pulchritudinous," I said, blushing. "You're an intelligent, pulchritudinous squirrel.

Now that I've embarrassed myself, I'll go make us some more almonds."

The two of them laughed hysterically.

"No, no. We're just pulling your tail, Rocky. The look on your face is hilarious," said Jewel, then gave me a big, celebratory kiss. "What does pulchritudinous mean?"

"It means pretty!" shouted Apple from the living room.

"That little Honeypot is a super genius. I love you all!" Sue-Ann said, giving me a firm hug. "Back to your comment. No, I'm not intimidated by chipmunks, nor squirrels, nor any other mammal, reptile, or bird that sits across from me in the courtroom. I believe in my work and myself. Which leads me to the second piece of information: your homework." She took out a book from her purse. "Directly from Mr. Fence. He wants you to read this book over the next week and write a full book report."

"A book report? You can't be serious," I said.

"As serious as a bullet ant sting," she replied, tossing the book on the countertop.

"Did you know a bullet ant sting is thirty times more painful than a Honeypot sting?" I mumbled.

"Rockford!" Jewel shouted in surprise, elbowing me in the chest again.

"What now?" I shrugged with embarrassment.

"A Honeypot sting?"

"Did I say Honeypot? I meant honeybee. Oh dear, where are those almonds?"

Jewel grabbed my arm, laughing, and kissed my cheek so hard her lipstick colored half my face. "Just teasing, lovepot. Sue-Ann, would you like some tea? Stay for a while," she wheedled.

"That's so sweet, but I have court in an hour. Raincheck?"

"It rains often, so I'll see you soon!" Jewel said, embracing Sue-Ann with a comforting hug.

"Today was a momentous victory. You all should celebrate! Oh, Rockford. Here's a note from Mr. Fence. He'll be in touch," said Sue-Ann, kissing my other cheek, then gave Jewel a big hug. "Bye, babies!"

"Bye!" voices yelled from the living room.

As she left, I looked inside the book. A handwritten note on Mulberry stationary fell out.

Rockford,

Congratulations on your legal victory today. It is both a milestone and a valuable lesson. This book, 'The Business Knack' was given to me by the author, Warner Buffingtail, when Mulberry went public. Mr. Buffingtail, a green iguana over a hundred years old, chronicles his account of running a successful candle company. Do me a kindness and read this over the next eight days. We'll regroup for a glorious, celebratory dinner. You deserve it.

Live long and blossom,

Billy Fence

I had read The Business Knack a few years ago. Mr. Buffingtail somewhat reminded me of Captain James T. with his etiquette—a masterful mix of charm and persistence. He famously wrote, "Noteworthy points in time occur after an 'aha moment,' where sudden insight strikes you like a lightning bolt. You must follow these aha moments to your success, no matter what path they take you on."

After rereading the book, I took a moment up on the roof to reflect on my life. As I gazed out to the vibrant nighttime forest, I got lost in the memories of my past self. It had been many moons since I sat amongst my siblings, wishing for enough food to come my way. Gone were the days when I ran carefree, learning how to cook with no responsibilities. The path I had taken was still new to me— the money, recognition, Jewel, our kids. Yet, I still felt like the same pup from Kona Valley; a cautious chipmunk with an urge to change the forest.

"Rockford, it's time we found your family," Jewel whispered, startling me from behind. "I read Mr. Buffingtail's book during my third year at Elderwood; I love aha moments. Your mother will be so happy to see you, to meet the kids, and me, of course. Aha!"

"She would absolutely adore you. But what if they don't want to be found? What if something bad happened to them?"

"Oh my golly! You're talking with too much lemon in those cheeks. You can't think like that. After dinner with Billy, you have nothing standing in your way. Rocky, you can literally fly on a hawk."

"You're right," I took a deep breath, "but—"

"No buts," she commanded. "Don't smush my aha moment, alright? You're finding the entire Honeypot scurry. Final decision as your wife, mother of your children, business partner, best friend, and everything in between!"

"My sunpot and my moonpot."

"And lovepot," she said, kissing me as we went back inside.

We agreed that after our celebratory dinner with Billy, I was going to find my mother once and for all. Nothing was going to stop us this time.

CHAPTER 20
A YEAR OF COURAGE

The following week, I completed my 'book report' for Billy—a thirty-five-page analysis of Warner Buffingtail's lengthy autobiography. I understood Billy was trying to prepare me for fame and success. As a token of appreciation for his support during the lawsuit, I bought him a special thank-you gift.

KNOCK. KNOCK. KNOCK!

I opened the door to Sue-Ann's big smile and compressing hug. She was wearing a brand-new gray suit that sparkled.

"Hello, Chef Honeypot! I love how clean your home is every single day!" She walked directly to the kitchen to eat roasted almonds.

"Thank you. Am I to assume you have plans for later tonight?" I asked.

She tottered back, almonds in cheeks. "Now, why would you think that?"

"Well, I appreciate your help this evening, but you're babysitting. I just assumed you'd wear something… less professional?"

"Is that Sue-Ann?" Jewel came in to hug her bestie.

After a moment of chit-chat between the two, Jewel elbowed me in the chest.

"Rocky, she is a professional. Don't judge based on Sue-Ann's wardrobe."

"Oh, my. That's not what I meant. What? No, it's just—I merely—"

The two burst out laughing again.

"We're just teasing, Rocky," said Jewel.

"All in good fun, sweetie," said Sue-Ann. "With this lawsuit behind us, we have unlimited opportunities ahead. I'm gonna be honest with you, Rockford. I think you've got a promising future. Mr. Fence believes in you and so do I. I'm here when you need me, and not because of these delicious almonds. Well, maybe just a little bit!"

"Isn't she just the best?" Jewel gushed.

Sue-Ann took a small container of lemon pie from her purse, handing it to Jewel.

"She is the best!" Jewel squealed, tears filling her eyes with joy as they embraced.

"Can you two please keep the glee to an appropriate decibel? Some of us are reading," hollered Apple from the other room.

Jewel elbowed me gently to stop me from chuckling.

"We know where she gets that tone, don't we?" Jewel whispered. "Watch that attitude, Apple!"

"I seriously love that little whiz kid," Sue-Ann laughed, raising her cup of water. "Let this evening be a start to a brand-new year. A year of courage to plant the acorns of your dreams so they one day become great oak trees that feed the forest. When you need an attorney, I'll be here!"

"Cheers to both ears!" I proclaimed.

"You're hired!" giggled Jewel. They hugged yet again.

I could feel the energy flowing throughout my body, energizing me like spring wildflowers. In a matter of seconds, I had my own *aha* moment. *A year of courage to plant my dreams of happiness.*

In response, I cheeped in a giddy fashion, giving Sue-Ann a big hug. "Help yourself to as many almonds as you'd like. This is the year of Honeypots! Thank you, Sue-Ann. You're a wonderful friend!"

"And an even better attorney. Thank you, Chef Honeypot! Have fun tonight, you two!"

That evening, we arrived at The Blue Butterfly, the restaurant where I had proposed to Jewel. As we walked into the decadent lounge, I held the book report in one paw and an orange gift-wrapped book in the other. I found myself admiring the updated decorations. It was visually stunning, yet the crowd still seemed a bit toffee-nosed pretentious for my taste.

Once again, the staff made us wear white covers on our hind paws to keep dirt and sod from their wooden floors.

"Rockford, my friend!" Billy welcomed me with a hug. "I'm so proud of you for coming out on top after your first lawsuit! A historic rite of passage in this neck-scratching corporate ecosystem."

I noticed nearly everyone in the lounge was looking at us. Billy had indeed become a larger-than-life celebrity. Consequently, he had improved his wardrobe wearing a slim-fitting green sweater.

"Thank you for being in our lives," Jewel proclaimed, giving him and Maude a warm hug.

"I can say the same for the both of you!" Billy continued.

"Life is full of random calculations, isn't it? Jewel, I hope you've kept this one far from nightshade berries."

"Very funny, Billy," I remarked.

"From now on, it's Mr. Fence."

"Oh. Alright, Mr. Fence. I'd like to—"

"I'm kidding! Ninety-nine percent of the forest now calls me Mr. Fence. They'll be calling you Mr. Honeypot sooner than later. Where is the maître d'? Time for dinner."

The maître d', a mouse dressed in a white tuxedo, approached us.

"Mr. Fence, sir. Your table is ready. Right this way," he said in a low, unimpressed voice.

We sat on the private rooftop terrace under dozens of graceful, multi-colored fireflies.

"It's beautiful," muttered Jewel, captivated by the twinkling glow.

"Isn't it? My life is so rich and wonderful these days," Maude whispered.

Then, as I looked over to my old pal, I placed the gift on the table. "Billy, I brought you a gift for helping us with the lawsuit. Oh, and here's the book report you requested."

"Rockford, I was joking about the book report!" Billy laughed, then sniffed the orange wrapping paper. "It feels like a book. A thick book. Botany? No, meteorology? Come on, we already know it will rain tomorrow."

As he opened the wrapped gift, he laughed.

A prized first edition of 'The Complete Adventures of Captain James T. Rockford.'

"Don't forget our roots, Billy. They keep us grounded," I said, nodding with respect.

"This is wonderful. Thank you! I just bought the exact same book for my daughter. Great minds think alike, don't they?"

"Oh dear. I could… I could get you something else?"

"No, no. I am humbled. Thank you," he replied, flagging down the waiter.

"Billy and I come here several times a week," said Maude, adjusting the table setting to her liking.

"Suddenly everyone wants to talk to me wherever we go. This is one of the only spots where we can dine in peace without interruptions," said Billy, waving at the busboy. "Excuse me, can we order some starters?"

A heavy-footed fellow scampered behind me.

"Sorry for the delay, we're short-staffed this evening. What can I do for you?" said a deep voice.

Jewel's eyes opened wide.

I know that voice.

Her jaw nearly dropped to the table.

"We'd love some lavender water and our waiter. Also, please put this book in the coat check. I'll grab it on our way out," said Billy, tossing the book over my head to the busboy.

As I turned around, I recognized a face I hadn't seen in a long time.

"Chuck?" I was shocked. "Chuck!"

Chuck blanched. "Nope. My name is… Maurice. I'll go alert the waiter that you're ready to order." He ran away.

I looked to Jewel in complete shock.

"Holy heavy leaf piles. That was Chuck!" I gasped.

"I know. I can't believe it!" she replied.

"Leaf piles aren't heavy. You know him?" Billy asked.

"Yes, he's an old friend of mine," I said.

"Go talk to him." Jewel nudged me.

"What do I say? He clearly doesn't want to talk."

"Do I sense some tension at the dinner table? I'll invite him back if you'd like a word." Billy got up from his seat. "I'll also find the waiter, just in case."

"No, no. Rockford will handle it," Jewel chimed in. "A year of courage, remember? It starts now. Go talk to him!"

I excused myself from the table to look for Chuck. I searched throughout the entire Blue Butterfly but couldn't find him. Our unfriendly mouse maître d' was no help either. He was busy with a party of twelve posh rabbits demanding a different table. There was only one way to find Chuck knowing it might hurt my chances of ever coming back here in the future.

I took the white covers off my paws and walked a few steps down the long hallway toward the ballroom, whistling with each step.

Only a matter of time now.

The maître d' dashed toward me. "Sir. Sir! SIR! I'm sorry, but you MUST keep paws covered indoors. It's our policy. We take pride in our policies."

"Oh, goodness me. They must have fallen off," I said, acting toffee-nosed. "Can you have someone fetch me a new pair?"

"Yes, sir. I'll send someone right away, sir."

Moments later, Chuck reluctantly approached me with a clean pair of paw covers.

"Here you are. A new set of paw covers," he mumbled.

"Chuck, I know it's you."

"I'm Maurice."

"Are you kidding me? Please don't do this."

"Don't do what? Steal your best friend's girlfriend, then marry her?"

"That's not what happened." I put my paw on his shoulder.

He took a big step backward.

"Is there a problem here?" asked the maître d'.

"Yes. I misplaced my pen. Can you please get me a pen?" I asked.

"Yes, sir. Right away, sir. Maurice, retrieve this chipmunk a pen."

As Chuck turned away, I grabbed his arm. To keep talking, I'd have to continue my toffee-nosed antics.

"Excuse me?" I said with a bite of tone. "I asked YOU to get me that pen. Blue ink, please."

The maître d' took offense but held his chin high. "Yes, sir. Right away, sir. One pen with blue ink."

"And a piece of paper," I said.

"And a piece of paper," he mumbled to himself as he walked away.

"Didn't know you turned into a toffee-nose chipmunk," grumbled Chuck.

"Oh, come on, that's not me. I'll do whatever it takes to talk with you!"

"Give Jewel back to me."

"What? We're married with five children."

"You… you have little Rockfords?" he asked, sniffling and wiping a tear from his eye.

"Yes. Four girls and one boy. Come to my tree-hut tomorrow. I've really missed you."

"Your pen with blue ink and one piece of paper," said the maître d', appearing suddenly once again.

"He needs another piece of paper," said Chuck.

I nodded my head yes.

"Yes, sir. Another piece of paper." The mouse's face turned two shades darker.

As he walked away, I wrote my address on the paper and gave it to Chuck.

"Tomorrow afternoon. We can work this out, I promise," I

said.

"For someone with glasses, you're very short-sighted, Rocky. I don't know how I feel about seeing Jewel again." He sniffled. "I almost leapt off the patio when I saw you two at the table."

"Life throws disappointments at us, but there's always two sides to every leaf. Have I told you the story of the tiger and the llama?"

"Yes."

"I did? No, no. I don't believe so."

"No, you didn't. I just don't wanna hear one of your la-dee-dah happy stories right now," he said, failing to hold back a smirk.

We paused for a brief moment, then erupted into laughter.

"Why are we laughing? It's a heartfelt story!" I wheezed.

"I have no idea," he replied, laughing with the same intensity.

Our laughter shifted to tears of joy until we collected ourselves.

"I'm happy you're safe. Please come tomorrow," I said, clearing my throat.

"Maybe. Maybe," he replied, walking away.

I stood in that hallway in order to take a few deep breaths. After all these years, Chuck had ended up working at The Blue Butterfly, of all places? I thought he had returned to the AMF, or was working in a bar somewhere, serving fermented crabapples. Regardless, he was safe, and it felt great to share such a genuine laugh with him after all these years.

"An additional piece of paper, sir." The maître d' returned, politeness masking his irritation.

"That will not be necessary. Thank you," I said, walking back toward the table.

He stood alone in the hallway, then hurled the paper at the wall. When he realized I was looking back at him, he gritted his teeth into a smile, picked up the paper, and scampered away.

CHAPTER 21
WINDS OF CHANGE

I woke up to the drumbeat of raindrops through the canopy leaves. It was five thirty in the morning; Jewel and the kids wouldn't wake up until seven. The air had a bitter chill, so I put on my long plum-colored sweats, comfy hoodie, and purple slippers.

The adventure to find my mother had been postponed another day or two with the sudden arrival of Chuck. Jewel and I were buzzing with curiosity, wondering what he'd been doing the past several years. *Why was he working at The Blue Butterfly? Why did he change his name to Maurice? Would he come over today?* Questions poured into my head faster than the raindrops above us.

The day flew by like the wind. Perhaps it was for the best, with the heavy clouds and intense rain. Sue-Ann and Jewel were in the living room with the kids enjoying chamomile tea while I gazed out the window, hoping for my long-lost buddy to arrive.

KNOCK. KNOCK. BANG! BANG!

"I'll get it!" I yelled, zipping to the front door.

I opened the door to see Chuck standing there soaking wet. He had definitely gained some weight over the years.

"You made it!" I shouted.

"Yeah. It was either come see you guys or sit on my sofa all evening. Should I shake outside or can I come in?"

"Outside. If you wouldn't mind, I—"

He shook his whole body violently, splattering me with grimy water until I smelled like wet Chuck.

For a few hours, we were all in a good mood. Chuck adored the children, especially Chester. He even promised to teach him how to hawk glide one day!

"I must admit, our last outing was a wee bit dramatic with the whole jumping-off-a-cliff moment," he said. "It worked out for the best, right? No regrets! Look at this wonderful family!"

Chuck smiled toward Sue-Ann. "And what a gorgeous attorney."

"Oh, stop." Sue-Ann blushed like a raspberry. "Do I smell cinnamon? Is it stick, powder, or leaf?"

"It's my natural aroma," he said with charm, slicking his hair back.

"But what happened after you left?" I interjected. "When did you start working at The Blue Butterfly?"

"I found myself back at the AMF, hawk-gliding with my old buddies. Protecting Tropland Rainforest was an honor of mine. They relieved me of my duties when I refused to accept a commission to be a ground general. Apparently, the laws state I'm too old to continue flying. Horseradish, as you would say. That's when an old pal connected me to The Blue Butterfly, where I work part-time saving up to start my own business."

"Did I hear new business?" Sue-Ann chimed in. "Do tell. I love the legality of start-ups."

Thunder struck in the distance. The storm had increased from a light drizzle to a heavy shower.

Our entire tree boomed with a rumble.

"Daddy!" Violet screamed, running to my leg.

"It's going to be okay," I said, petting her head. "It's just a rainstorm. We get them all the time, do you remember?"

Trees crackled across the forest as the winds picked up.

"Rockford? Come close," cried Jewel, holding Olive and Lily. Violet and Chester were now glued to my side.

"It's going to be alright, everyone. Our brain is reacting to fear, triggering our nervous response," Apple said.

Then came the sound of nearby tree-huts being smashed by debris.

"Daddy!" Apple leaped into my arms.

In an instant, all the lights shut off while the tree began to shudder as though we were having an earthquake.

Sue-Ann grabbed on to Chuck's arm.

"Jewel! Can you hear me?" I yelled.

"Barely!" she yelled back. "I think this is a hurricane! We need to get to the safety-hut!"

"Take the kids and Sue-Ann to our drop lift. We'll lower you down to the safety-hut and meet you there. Chuck, where are you? Come with me!" I yelled as we made our way toward the top floor.

The winds were escalating faster with each passing second. I opened a latch to reveal the rope wrapped tightly around a branch.

"This rope will lower them down to the safety-hut. On the count of three, help me unwrap and lower them down!" I yelled.

Another bolt of lightning struck too close for comfort. Half the roof ripped off my tree-hut!

The sudden blast of wind lifted me off my hind paws, throwing me against the wall.

"Rocky!" Chuck yelled. His extra weight kept him grounded.

"Unhook the rope for the drop lift!" I screamed, trying to get back up.

He grabbed my arm and pulled me to the rope. We both used all of our strength to fight against the strong winds. Thankfully, Chuck was able to unhook the rope from the wall, enabling us to lower everyone down safely.

"We have to get down to the base of the tree!" I shouted, cringing from a sharp pain in my shoulder.

"Here! Take this rope!" he yelled, throwing extra rope my way. "We'll climb down together. Grab my paw!"

Flashes of Sora flickered in my head.

I remembered the look on her face years ago during the storm at Eight Poem Garden.

I could hear my voice, *grab my paw,* as she stared at me on the edge of extinction.

My heart beat faster.

Breathing became more difficult.

Faster.

The pain from my shoulder was radiating up my neck toward my cheek.

"Rocky! Rocky! Snap out of it! Grab my paw and tie this rope around you!" Chuck bellowed.

I froze, motionless as a wounded caterpillar.

He tied the rope around my waist, then slapped me across the cheek.

"Snap out of it!"

The rainfall was so intense that the drops felt like I was being punched over and over. As we made our way toward the bottom of the tree, I slipped on a wet leaf. Trying to catch my grip, my nails ripped through the tree bark as I flew off into the darkness. My body swung around through the canopy until a tight pull squeezed my stomach. The rope saved me just short of a pointy, broken tree branch.

Chuck pulled me back on to the tree. "You alright? We're almost there, Rocky!"

Once at the safety-hut, we opened the door, leapt inside, and immediately locked the door behind us.

"Rockford! Chuck!" Jewel ran to us.

Two lamps provided light. We were buried deep enough inside the tree trunk that the winds couldn't reach us.

My heart was pounding, my cheeks were frozen. I was covered in parasite-infested mud with the worst rope burn across my waist and a shoulder that was super sore. In the past, I would have felt a wave of anxiety from such events. Now I was much stronger than I used to be. All that mattered was the safety of my family.

"Oh my golly! Rocky, your arm!" Jewel shouted.

"Yes. It hurts more than it looks."

"I got you, Rocky," said Chuck, grabbing my arm and yanking it downwards.

POP!

I yelped louder than a red fox.

"There you are. Feel better?" he asked.

"Remarkably, yes," I said, ready to faint as the tree shook even harder.

All we could do was wait until the hurricane passed.

CHAPTER 22
TROPLAND REDEFINED

I sat in the dark, still as a slug, holding my family. Their sleepy wheezing soothed my nerves despite the howling wind.

The storm had passed by early morning. Sunlight burned my eyes as I cracked open the door. At first glance, the force of lightning had split through the canopy trees, destroying Tropland's power grids, tree-huts, and the natural order of our forest. I couldn't see far past the broken tree-huts tossed around our land like a green salad. Our beautiful new green-huts were completely torn apart, shredded by the storm. A stream of muddy water flowed across the land where they once stood.

Our tree had broken in half.

Our tree-hut was obliterated.

Thankfully, we were unharmed. Our safety-hut had been built high enough on the tree not to be submerged under the water.

"Over there, Rocky! That tree is the highest point in the

canopy. Let's get a better view to assess the wreckage," said Chuck.

"Everyone stay put. We'll be right back," I told my worn-out family.

I noticed my purple amethyst lodged between soaked leaves on a branch.

How did it fall out of my pocket?

I put it back in my pocket and followed Chuck, sprinting across the broken branches. On our way, Chuck and I helped several families out of their wreckage. One particular chipmunk family was trapped under a broken tree branch with no visible way out except for a small hole to yell "help" through.

"Dad!" Chester shouted, following from behind.

"Chester? I told you to stay put," I said.

"Rocky, we could use the help. Saving these chipmunks needs more muscle," said Chuck.

"Mom said I can help. Please, Dad? I'm wearing a shirt!" Chester pleaded.

"Okay, but be careful," I said, jumping from tree to tree, "and make sure you use your hind legs to grip safely."

THUMP!

THUMP!

A group of forty-three wild pigs racing through the flooded wreckage broke through the debris on our right side.

"RAMPAGE!" Chuck boomed. "Hold on to something!"

"CHESTER! NO!" I screamed as he slipped off the branch into the muddy water.

"DAD!" he yelled back, swimming to avoid the stampede of pigs.

I wanted to jump in after him but I kept losing sight with each passing hog. Every time he came up for air, he was thrown back down by the force of the water.

"I'm going to jump in!" I yelled.

"You'll be squashed, Rocky!" Chuck exclaimed. "Too dangerous!"

"I don't care. Chester! Daddy's coming for you!"

Out of the trees came a large, dark-haired gibbon swinging from branch to branch. The small ape leapt from pig to pig, looking around for Chester.

"I see him!" he shouted in a deep voice, leaning over while holding onto the large, elongated tooth of a pig.

He grabbed Chester, lifting him out from the murky water unharmed.

"Be more careful," he said, tossing Chester into my outstretched arms. "The forest is a mess."

"Thank you so much!" I shouted. My heart was pounding.

"Yeah, thanks!" said Chuck. "Can you help these folks? They're in a bind."

The gibbon pushed over the tree branch in order to save the chipmunks.

"Thanks again." I nodded, eyes watering. "Is there anything we can do for you? Anything you need?"

"I'm off to my family. Pay it forward," he said.

"Yes. We will! Thank you!" I replied, holding Chester, who was shivering.

The gibbon nodded as he ran off out of sight.

"What's 'pay it forward'?" asked Chester.

"It means do something nice for someone else. Like he just did for us."

As far as our eyes could see, the forest had received considerable damage.

Chuck suddenly turned pale, nearly losing his balance.

"You alright?" I asked.

"No. I'll be back in a bit. Need to check on my tree-hut." He jumped away from one tree branch to another.

"Chuck. Wait!" I said, but it was no use.

He was gone. *Again.*

We spent the rest of the week cleaning, organizing, and sanitizing our safety-hut. We also reached out to those whose tree-huts were destroyed, sharing our basic supplies. The food supply of Tropland had been ripped apart, scattered, and crushed with the storm's mighty weight. For many, the only refuge was to stay at one of Tropland's nine local shelter-domes built for emergency shelter. We were fortunate to find comfort in our own safety-hut.

Each night at bedtime, Jewel fell asleep in my arms, the kids tucked around us. Everything we had built was gone. Our home, our green-huts, our way of life. The rainforest was feeling melancholy; the insects, frogs, and monkeys were singing songs of sadness.

As the rain started falling once again, the thunder crackled in the distance. I held up my amethyst stone to the lamp, gazing at the beautiful purple color. My eyes were dry with the sting and exhaustion of being awake for many days in a row. This was a sign that I needed to refill my motivation—a sign that told me there is always light, even in darkness. Nothing is ever perfect; the seed of happiness grows from within us. The following day was my birthday, but my only wish wasn't for more paw soap. My wish was to have the courage to balance the branches of my life, to find serenity for my Honeypots.

CHAPTER 23
BIRTHDAY WISH

No matter the struggles, some things will never change. The sun will rise every morning, the rivers will continue to flow with life, and the vines will resume their never-ending quest to climb toward the sun.

As long as my heart continues to beat, one more fact remains true every year: October Eighth is my birthday. Before everyone woke up, I sat by myself on the top of our broken tree stump, staring out in to the forest. The EFE (Emergency First Elephants) finally arrived to bulldoze the debris. Without their help, within less than a month, the foul smell of algae would be overwhelming, and the natural decay of our ecosystem would make this grove uninhabitable.

Again, I was reminded of Sora and the monks. The last time I'd seen a storm of this magnitude was at Eight Poem Garden. I wondered if the monks were back safe, if Sora was healed. That chapter of my life felt like a lifetime ago.

"How do you feel this morning?" asked Jewel, climbing

toward me with a cup of hot tea.

"Still a bit sore. My left knee makes an odd clicking sound when I jump."

"Always something with you, lovepot. I made you a special tea blend. Chamomile, cardamom seeds, ginger, honey, and lemon. Happy Birthday!" She handed it to me with a kiss.

"It's delightfully balanced," I said, savoring each sip. "Cheers."

She took a few steps back, crossing her arms. "What's wrong? Is your knee bothering you that badly? How is your shoulder? Your ribs? Is it Chuck? Your mother?"

"Nothing is wrong." I giggled at her dramatic intensity.

"I know you, Honeypot. What's wrong?"

"I love you," I said, bringing her close to me. "I promise we're going to rebuild our tree-hut as magnificent as it was before. Perhaps even better. It's just… this is the second time I've witnessed the demolition of green-huts. I thought about utilizing a dome structure for future use, but it's not possible with our ventilation and glass panels. They are just too vulnerable.

"Rocky." She put her paw over my mouth.

"Mhmm?" I mumbled.

"Stop worrying. We'll figure it out."

The monkeys above us continued acting like hooligans, fighting amongst themselves. With every croad, strut, and groat they made, I got more and more restless.

"I know things are bad. Terrible, actually," she continued, still holding her paw over my mouth. "But our safety-hut worked like a charm because of YOU! You wanted us to be safe, and we are safe. You, lovepot, do the impossible. Today is your birthday, so let's celebrate!"

"How did I get so lucky?" I mumbled through her paw.

"Your spicy good looks." She grabbed my paw. "By the way, I know it doesn't feel like the right time, but I think we need to find your family. A storm of this size brings the forest together."

"What about the kids?" I said, shaking my head. "It's too dangerous."

"I'm coming with you!" Chester's head appeared from beneath the branch as he climbed up toward us. "Happy Birthday, Dad! I'm paying it forward for your birthday."

"Happy Birthday, Daddy. I'm coming, too," Apple added from behind Chester.

"Thank you for the birthday wishes. You're not coming with me. Chester, remember what happened the other day?"

"Come on! That was an accident," complained Chester. "I'm not afraid."

"As Mom says, when life gives you lemons, make lemon sorbet," said Apple.

"Or lemon pie," chimed Chester.

"Or lemon sorbet with lemon pie!" countered Apple.

"Chester and Apple could help. We're perfectly fine in our indestructible safety-hut," Jewel said. "Now is the perfect time to visit the nearest dome. Sue-Ann and I will watch over Lily, Violet, and Olive for a few days. You know, it wouldn't hurt to bring a few of your brothers back with you. We could use their help putting things back in order."

The monkeys above screamed and scrambled off toward another tree.

THUMP!

Chuck dropped down on the branch beside me, nearly knocking everyone over.

"Can you believe those loudmouth primates?" He hugged me as best as he could while holding a grocery bag. "They thought they could take this away? Not from me and not on your birthday! Happy Birthday, Rocky. Good morning, Honeypots."

"It's Chuck!" Chester bounced, giving him a fist bump.

Chuck handed me a bag filled with blueberries, raspberries, and a few peanuts.

"Thank you! Everything alright back at your hut?" I asked.

"Oh no, no, no. The whole grove of trees snapped like twigs! If you think it's bad here in Elderwood, it's much, much worse where I live. Good thing I was with you last night, or I'd be peanut butter!"

"Oh, dear. Come to think of it, Chuck, if you weren't here to help with the rope, we'd be peanut butter as well. Thank you!" I replied, hugging the big guy.

"Hazelnut butter would be more appropriate," observed Apple.

"True." Chuck laughed. "Things happen for a reason, right? Anyway, what's the plan?"

"We're going to find Grandma Honeypot at one of the shelter-domes," said Apple, picking dirt from Chester's head. "Mom only gave us two days. Given the distance we'll need to travel, the probability of finding Grandma increases if we hawk-glide. Can you teach us, Uncle Chuck?"

"Uncle Chuck?" His voice cracked. "I'm an uncle?"

"Think about it, lovepot." Jewel grasped my paw. "Now is the perfect time to find them!"

"But first, let's eat. Birthdays make me hungry!" Chuck shouted, walking back toward our safety-hut.

We had a celebratory birthday breakfast that morning. The whole group huddled around and sang Happy Birthday in the cutest, most off-beat tune. Little Lily had the hiccups, Chester had peanuts stuffed in his cheeks, Olive and Violet competed over who could sing louder, and Apple sang in a foreign bird language.

I loved every second of it.

A few hours later, we regrouped on the branch with a pencil and a large piece of paper in order to lay out the details.

"The plan is simple," I said, surrounded by Jewel, Sue-Ann, Chuck, and my pint-sized Honeypots. "During a catastrophic storm, most animals find refuge in a shelter-dome. There are only nine shelter-domes across Tropland, two of which are within range of Rica Canyon. Our only hope is that they made it safely to one of those two domes and that they are still there. The nearest dome is Agoura, South of Kona Valley, where I grew up. Traveling by hawk should take us two hours or less. If they aren't there, we fly east to Serenity Falls, another two- to three-hour flight. Best case scenario: we split up on two hawks and return back safely. Worst case scenario: we return home empty-pawed in good spirits because we will always have each other."

"Live long and blossom, Rocky." Jewel kissed my cheek. "Two days. Not a stick longer."

"Be safe, Cinnamon." Sue-Ann kissed Chuck's cheek.

He looked at me with that smile I hadn't seen in years.

Just to be safe, our bags were packed with enough gear and supplies for five days. As we hiked toward the tallest tree, Chuck explained the specifics of hawk-gliding to Apple and Chester.

On one paw, we were on a journey to find my family after so many years of separation. On the other, I was watching my firstborn daughter and only son hike up a tree to hawk-glide for the first time! This was a lot to chew on.

Arriving at the base of the tree, Chester and Apple stayed close while Chuck created the fire diversion. Thick, gray smoke filled the air. Soon enough we heard the loud squawk of a large red-tailed hawk.

"It's not a great black hawk, but we don't have time to wait," said Chuck. "On my mark, Honeypots. Ready?"

We got in formation, ready to sprint up the tree when Chuck put the fire out. The large hawk squawked loudly above the canopy, scaring all the smaller birds from the trees. Even a couple monkeys screamed in terror and swung out of the way.

"One… two… three!" Chester yelled.

"Go time!" Chuck shouted.

We climbed toward the beast where it perched in the trees, looking down at the thick, black smoke.

We all jumped at the same time, landing on the hawk, who flew up through the treetops with a loud cry. Chuck pulled the hawk's neck feathers in the direction of Kona Valley, and we were off!

The temperature drastically dropped as we punched through the canopy to the open sky. Clenching tightly to the feathers, we all examined the damaged rainforest. From the bird's-eye-view we were finally able to see the aftermath of the storm. Poor Tropland was still struggling to sprout a new beginning.

Two hours later, we arrived near the Agoura dome. We could barely move from flying through the stinging cold wind. Much like Elderwood, this section of the forest had felt the full force of the storm. Fortunately, the massive shelter-dome was built against several dozen giant sequoia trees reinforced with the same iron bark as our safety-hut.

Chuck stuck his finger in the hawk's ear to land us safely upon a coconut tree. From the base of the tree, we braved our way through the rough terrain toward the dome, encountering booming monkey howls, icy winds, and glares from large, hungry animals roaming the duff.

Tropland's Emergency Response was noticeably faster here than back home. Inside the dome all the occupants were organized into height and weight groups, easing confusion. The larger animals settled in the lower deck while the smaller animals took a ramp, climbed, or flew to the upper deck.

We made our way up the ramp holding paws. You can imagine the heat brewing within this giant, wooden dome. There were so many various species in one location. We heard every hoot, holler, scuttle, bleat, croak, roar, buzz, and honk as we continued walking.

"Did you just hear a honk?" Chuck asked.

"Yes. It's just a goose," I said.

"Actually, Daddy, it sounds like a male. Which would be a gander, not a goose," Apple said.

"Hot diggity. You got yourself a mini Rockford!" Chuck remarked.

We searched the upper deck of the dome for hours with no luck. It smelled strongly of peanuts, the primary snack being handed out by friendly rabbit volunteers. A sight I'll never forget, families of all shapes and sizes huddled together for safety.

Chester broke away from us several times throughout the day to pass out roasted hazelnuts to families in need. His way of paying it forward was heartwarming. We couldn't get mad at his kindness but needed to make sure our rations were adequate.

"I don't think they're here," Chuck finally said once the sun began to fade. "Let's rest up and leave early in the morning."

"Wait. We're staying here?" Chester questioned, nibbling on a hazelnut.

"It's filthy," cried Apple, taking each step with care. "Pass the paw sanitizer, please."

"I packed masks! Three purple and one blue." I handed the blue mask to Apple along with the paw sanitizer.

"Good thinking, Daddy."

"That's a bit much, Rocky. We'll be fine," said Chuck dismissively, sitting on the floor next to our bags.

"I'll be fine too, Dad." Chester said, "Apple, don't be such a scaredy-snail."

"I'm not scared!" She sanitized a small area to lay down on. "I'm just cautious."

CHAPTER 24
SEARCH AND RESCUE

The sticky humidity woke us at sunrise. Heaps of insects were buzzing around us like they were part of a parade.

Fortunately, we spotted a great black hawk with unique purple tail feathers. Perched high up on a coconut tree, the giant hawk was watching over Agoura as if planning its breakfast menu. This was our one-way ticket to Serenity Falls. Step by step, the four of us followed hawk-gliding protocol as we made our way onto the back of the great raptor. Unlike other hawks, his feathers felt as soft as silk pajamas. As we held on tight, he soared through the damaged canopy with such speed that every piece of dust, moss, and speck of dirt from the shelter-dome flew right off of us!

"Hold on!" I shouted to Apple and Chester, who were both enjoying every second of this thrill ride.

It should have taken us three hours to fly to Serenity Falls, but on this hawk, we arrived in thirty minutes. There was still noticeable damage to the forest, but not as much as in other parts of Tropland. All the power lines were still down and most of the duff was covered with debris and muddy leaves. At least several tree-huts and restaurants in the area were still standing.

After we dismounted from our speedy hawk, the four of us approached the entrance to the Serenity Falls shelter-dome. Our bodies still shivering from the icy altitudes of flying, we noticed all sorts of apes patching up the dome's many cracks. A herd of large mammals cleared out broken trees and large debris from the surrounding area.

"Whoa, whoa. Are those mooses?" asked Chester, pointing to the massive animals.

"No, those are the great okapi. A relative of the giraffe without the long necks… and don't point; it's rude," I said.

"Plus, it's moose, not mooses. Don't you know anything about zoology?" Apple reprimanded Chester, turning her attention to the okapi. "Good morning, y'all!"

"Is that a chipmunk?" one of the okapi spoke out with a thick accent as he bent down toward us. "What a mighty voice you have. Good morning, young chipmunk." His voice vibrated through our bodies.

"You get along with everyone, don't you?" Chuck remarked, rubbing Apple's head.

"I'm very likeable," she replied.

As we entered the dome, we were met by a diverse group of animals tending to each other. Some prepared meals, others addressed those with injuries, and all seemed to be conversing with one another. The critters here at Serenity Falls were in much better moods than those in Agoura.

As we hiked up to the top deck, we noticed a group of animals were huddled in the corner.

"What's going on?" Chuck asked a cream-colored rabbit.

"New shipment of wood comin' in today," she answered.

"Says we're getting it free to rebuild our huts! What a day. Our prayers have been answered!"

All the animals applauded once again as they separated down different hallways, each holding green tickets.

My head scanned each face faster than a woodpecker pecking a tree.

Where are you, Mother?

As I turned, scanning the deck, I saw Chester being harassed by a suspicious chipmunk three times his size, wearing a dark hoodie.

"Chester!" I shouted, running toward them.

The chipmunk had Chester's bag in one paw and was pushing him in the face with the other.

"Give them back to me!" Chester squealed. "Dad! This nig-nog is stealing my nuts!"

Chuck barrel rolled through the crowd and punched the attacker in the nose, taking back the bag. "Leave my boy alone," he snarled, fist still in the air.

The chipmunk picked up a few roasted hazelnuts from the ground, then ran off crying.

Chester and Apple both gave Chuck a hug. "Thanks, Uncle Chuck."

"Well I'll be a porcupine's uncle. If it isn't the triumphant Rockford T. Honeypot and his gang of bullies," said a voice from behind us.

I knew that obnoxious voice.

Braxton McFudden clapped his paws. He was wearing a crisp black suit, and had a crew of raccoons surrounding him, all wearing 'McFudden Staff' T-shirts.

"Good morning, Braxton. Nice to see you again," I said sarcastically.

"So, you just waltz in here and punch these poor folks of

Serenity Falls?" he remarked, eyeing Chuck and the kids. "On behalf of this community, which will be entirely rebuilt by McFudden's finest lumber, your attitude is not welcome."

"Braxton, we mean no quarrel. I'm here looking for my family and that's it."

"And I'm here building my new business!" he hissed. "Since you bankrupted my company, I had to start over."

"Mind your own business, Braxton," I said walking away from his loud mouth, "we have nothing to discuss here."

Braxton and his band of raccoons followed us down the ramp. "How's Jewel doing these days? We should all grab a meal once we finish rebuilding McFudden Hotel."

The suspicious chipmunk thief approached us, holding a handkerchief up to his bloody nose.

"Rockford? Is that you?"

"Back off." Chuck grabbed him by his hoodie.

"It's me, Clarence. Rockford's brother!"

Chuck pulled his hood down. I couldn't believe it! It really was my brother!

He gave me a hug so intense, I felt some of my ribs shifting.

"Clarence? Oh dear, Clarence!" I gasped. "Where is everyone?" I shouted.

"Same ol' Rockford, asking questions."

"Clarence, why were you stealing my son's bag?"

"You got a son? He was passin' out nuts an' I wanted more."

"Looks like we got the whole family back together, huh?" Braxton sneered, picking his nails. "How long has it been, Rockford? Twenty years or so since you were stranded back in Kona Valley? This is a historic moment, isn't it? I saw Emma about an hour ago."

"Clarence!" I said, grabbing his hoodie. "Where—are—

they?"

"Mom and Pops are over there by the fire pits. You still the same goody two-shells Rockford, aren't ya? At least this feller is givin' us free wood instead of punchin' me in the nose."

"Sorry for punching your brother," Chuck muttered as we walked toward a set of fire pits.

Squirrels, rabbits, raccoons, mice, and other animals huddled safely by five large fire pits. Each fire had a certified badger standing guard to ensure safety. Can you imagine the destruction a wildfire would cause in a giant, wooden dome? Public fires were taken very seriously.

"Excuse us. We're trying to get through," I said, holding Apple and Chester by their paws.

Chuck moved critters out of the way until a dozen chipmunks approached us.

I couldn't believe my eyes.

"Is that you, Rockford?" asked one of my brothers.

"Rockford?" another Clarence shouted.

"Did you say a doctor?" said another brother.

"Doctor who?" asked a fourth Clarence.

"It's Rockford!" shouted another.

Each Clarence gave me a hug, one after another. Clarence after Clarence, as if it had only been a few moons since we last spoke. All of them looked so much older than what I expected. They say you are what you eat; these fellas must have been eating filth for some time.

Had it really been that long?

The group of Clarences moved out of the way in order to give me a clear view of my father as he stood by the fire, staring at me. He had aged worse than a sour raisin, now using a wooden cane to keep himself balanced. The shadows on my father's face flickered with a sinister light from the radiant fire.

In his paw was one of my roasted hazelnuts, which he was examining between the glares.

"Yer brother gave me this a minute ago. This yers?" he asked, coughing.

"Yes," I replied, intimidated by the old-timer who had troubled me as a child.

"This yer son, too?"

"Who's the geezer?" Chester whispered to Chuck.

"Yes," I replied to my father. "Chester. Apple. This is your grandfather, Clarence."

"What you did is a disgrace to the Filbert nut, okay? They're meant to be eaten raw, as Mother Nature intended." He tossed the nut to the floor. "Clarences, we got buildin' to do!"

"Oh, true you are, Clarence. These huts don't build themselves, now, do they?" Braxton joked.

"No, they do not. An' I ain't movin' anytime soon, so let's get to werk!" My father hobbled away with his cane.

"Free wood for free labor. New laws of the forest, according to the McFudden contract," boomed Braxton. "I provide the lumber, the town becomes the workforce. Everyone wins and lives happily ever after in their luxurious, McFudden-owned properties. Serenity Falls, or McFudden Falls," he snickered with an evil laugh. "Until next time, Rockford."

"Got that right." My father continued to hobble away. "Next time."

"Stop right in those tracks, Clarence! If you take one more step, I'll snap that cane faster than a cracked filbert!" a voice yelled from behind my brothers.

I knew that voice! One I had waited years to hear!!

Like a snowflake descending from the tree-tops, my mother arrived with watery eyes. She stopped short when she saw

Apple and Chester holding paws, the tears ran down her cheeks. Though my father and brothers had aged with time, my mother looked just as graceful as I remembered.

"Would you look at these adorable Honeypots," she stopped for a moment to catch her breath. "I've waited so long to see you, my Captain Rockford T."

"Mother!" I hugged her as every muscle in my body relaxed for the first time in a long while.

Chester and Apple joined in, wrapping their arms around our waists.

"You look just like your Grand-daddy Clarence," she said to Chester, bonking my father over the head with her paw. "I knew we'd have grand-babies one day, Clarence!"

"Family hug!" laughed Chuck, wrapping his arms around us.

"This is our friend, Chuck," I explained.

My mother sniffed. "Do I smell cinnamon?"

"Uncle Chuck loves his cinnamon!" announced Chester.

Braxton strutted toward us. "I hate to break up this reunion, but like the old chipmunk said, these huts don't build themselves. We've got work to do, citizens of Serenity Falls! Let's get back to work!"

My mother, tired of Braxton's nonsense, stomped her hind paw. "Braxton, your mouth is just as big as it was when you were a spoiled little pup. Nobody is stopping you or your raccoon thugs from building these huts. Bug off!"

Braxton mumbled something surly but nodded to his raccoon crew. They all walked back down the hallway.

Apple climbed up my mother's flowing blue dress and into her arms. "Hi, Grandma. My name is Apple, and this is Chester."

Chester smiled, wagging his tail. "Hiiii."

"Wanna know how to say 'nice to meet you' in a native bat dialect?" Apple asked, then screeched loudly in our ears.

"You are the cutest chipmunk I have ever seen," gushed my mother, then looked down at Chester. "And you? I could eat you up like a couple of oak nuts! Come sit with me. We have so much to catch up on." She turned, as if remembering my father, and yelled after him, "Clarence! Don't go hobbling too far!"

He waved his cane around irritably.

She looked deep into my eyes with the same unconditional love I had felt as a child. "I left you once before. I will not do it again. Where have you been all these years?"

"First and foremost, I have something for you." I pulled the purple amethyst stone from my pocket. "Beauty is everywhere. Sometimes you just need to look from a different angle."

"You remembered?" She wiped tears from her cheeks.

"I remember everything. As for my adventures, we have so much to discuss! Let's start with Eve at the Evening Musk."

-Back to Green-Hut Market 39-

Theo can't believe his eyes as a large black hawk with purple tail feathers descends through the treetops.

SQUAAAAAWK!

Perching on a large branch above the crowd, the great beast shocks most of the animals gathered around Rockford, captivated by his story.

A hefty muskrat wearing a large straw hat dismounts the hawk, followed by a half-dozen smaller muskrats. They all hold paws as they walk toward Rockford.

Randy bounces on his tail with sheer excitement after noticing a brown AMF jacket on the hefty muskrat. "Hey! It's

Uncle Chuck!"

"Hey! It's the famous monkey on the livestream!" Chuck laughs in response, giving Randy a fist bump.

Chuck has aged over the years and now has a patch of gray fur on his chin. He lifts Rockford off the ground in a great embrace.

"Look who decided to return after all this time!" Chuck shouts, followed by a great belly laugh. "Welcome home, Captain!"

"You look much older than I imagined," observes Randy.

An elderly female squirrel in a fancy gray suit approaches.

"And you must be?" Randy asks.

"Sue-Ann Goldblum. Nice to meet you." She strides up to Rockford. "Hello, my dearest friend. I've missed you profoundly."

Theo races up Rockford's back to his shoulder. "Wait. Goldblum? You two got married? Spoilers!"

"I've missed you both very much," says Rockford with a soft voice.

Holly hovers above to film their close exchange.

"Sue-Ann," Rockford whispers as they embrace, "forgive me for not staying in touch. Apple has been keeping me in the loop."

"No apologies needed, darling. I'm so happy you're back!" She gives him a final squeeze. "We brought our family to hear the rest of your story. May we join you?"

"Totally!" Theo speaks up. "New fans for my yo-yo routine," he says under his breath with a crafty smile.

"Theo, you remind me so much of your grandfather, Chester, when he was your age," says Sue-Ann fondly, patting his head.

A few of the animals closest to Rockford make room for

the new group of muskrats.

"Did you tell the story about the spooky swamplands?" asks Chuck.

"No, not yet," Rockford replies.

"Ladies and gents, I present the muskrat in a straw hat! The one and only Chuck Goldblum and his wife Sue-Ann have just arrived at Green-Hut Market 39!" Holly says to the camera. "The comments section is lighting up like fireflies in springtime. Keep the hearts coming, Tropland. Rockford, you're not gonna believe this, but we've got two million, six hundred thousand and twelve critters watching *live*!"

"Heyoooo, Tropland!" belts one of Chuck's grandchildren to the camera, jumping up onto his grandfather's lap.

"Rockford, meet Rocky the third," Chuck introduces him.

"A pleasure to meet you, Rocky the third," says Rockford, shaking the young boy's paw.

"Now that we're here, let's start over. We didn't start watching until you made it to Sora and the mindful monks," says Chuck.

The crowd ripples with disbelieving mutters.

"Chuck, we've been at this for a while now," Rockford replies awkwardly. "I was telling everyone about the aftermath of the great storm."

Chuck lets out a great belly-laugh. "I'm pulling your tail! So, you haven't gotten to Ergo and the swamplands?" He elbows the weasel next to him with excitement. "This is great, isn't it?"

The poor weasel tumbles over into a leaf pile. Rosalina, seated nearby, helps him up and dusts him off.

CHAPTER 25
MOVING FORWARD

I talked with my mother until twilight, recounting every adventure I had written in my journal over the past two decades.

"Thank you," she said, holding my paw. "For never giving up on me or your dreams to travel the forest frontier. I knew you'd find your unshelled diamond. And there's so much more yet to happen!"

Nestled together by the fire pits, we all slept like koala bears that whole night. It was such a cozy feeling, despite the unsanitary floors and high levels of humidity. I felt a shimmer of excitement at the idea of returning to Jewel with my mother.

The first one to wake up in the early morning, I was mid-yawn when the scent of someone's terrible coffee-grass breath hit my nostrils.

"Good morning," Braxton whispered, kneeling toward my whiskers. He held my journal in his paws. "Got a moment to chat?"

I swiftly grabbed the journal from him, jumping up. "Why do you have this?" I snapped back. "Did you read it?"

"Not all of it, but I'd like to discuss these green-huts of yours. I think we can make a lot of money together."

"Come with me." I grabbed his arm and pulled him away from where everyone else lay sleeping peacefully. "Are you nuts? You don't just take something that isn't yours. Well, perhaps 'you' do, as history indicates, but this is personal!"

"Listen, I'm not one to break up a family. You Honeypots are experts in that field. I'm gonna need one of two things from you. Either we discuss a partnership with McFudden Enterprises to supply lumber for these new green-huts—I've copied your blueprints from that journal, by the way—or I'll need all paws on deck building out the community until its completion. I'll leave it to you to make the right decision."

"What's going on here?" my mother asked, rubbing her sleepy eyes.

"You all signed the contract, Emma." He shrugged. "Don't pit me as the bad chipmunk here."

Yet another reason I've always disliked Braxton.

"This is horseradish! They're not going to work for you! They're coming to Elderwood with me," I steamed.

"We are?" my mother asked.

"Not a problem, Rockford T. Moneybags." Braxton picked lint from his jacket with a smug look on his face. "You'll need to pay off the balance of their lumber in full. Then we'll discuss our green-hut blueprints. I have some thoughts of my own that could help with expansion."

As I looked to my mother, whom I hadn't seen in what felt like a lifetime, she placed her paws on my cheeks. "Sweetheart, I can't leave your father."

"You don't have to leave anyone ever again! You're all

coming to Elderwood with me."

Braxton picked the final piece of lint from his jacket. "Don't be so foolish, Rockford. We have contracts in place and abide by the laws that govern them."

"Pygmy goats have more respect for the laws than you! We'll discuss this later" I snarled, walking back to my family.

Later that morning, after a cup of ginger and mint tea, we gathered outside to prepare for our journey back to Elderwood. The sun lit up the canopy, no wind, no clouds, and no rain. Unfortunately, the heat and humidity levels were so far above an acceptable tolerance that my ears were radiating heat from my body like fire pits.

My father, gloomy-looking as I'd always remembered, was busy with my brothers, lifting and fastening wooden planks onto a transport goose.

"We're all going to Elderwood," I said with my head held high. "Don't worry, I'm not going to leave you stranded like a certain someone did to me years ago. I'll negotiate your contracts with Braxton and take care of it. Then, you'll come back to live with us. Deal?"

"Who do you think you are, spittin' those chubby cheeks at me? We don't want yer money an' we ain't going nowhere, okay? No deal."

My mother kicked my father's cane out from under his arm. "Clarence!"

Suddenly, a jaguar growled from the trees nearby, frightening Chester, who grabbed on tightly to my leg.

"Got yer boy scared of noises like you, eh?" My father tried laughing but nearly coughed up his breakfast. "You haven't changed since you were his age, have ya? Go on home, Rockford. Okay?"

My mother picked up Chester in her arms. "These are your

grandchildren! Clarence, what's wrong with you?"

"Me? Did yer mother tell you about yer brothers and sisters?" He glared at us. "Why don't you ask about our lives instead of blabbing 'bout yerself all day an' night?"

A surge of anxiety rushed through my body.

Why did my father suddenly look even more miserable?

The entire time we'd been here, I'd only talked about myself. I didn't think to ask how my parents were doing, why my sisters weren't with us, why only a third of my brothers were here, or what they'd been up to all these years. *How could I have been so selfish?*

As my mother sat down beside me, her breath was shallow with grief. She placed her paw on my shoulder, explaining how they'd lost the majority of my siblings in the great fire of Rica Canyon years ago. My surviving sisters had all gotten married, had babies, and moved on with their lives living halfway across the forest. Out of the thirty-six Clarence boys only twelve remained, none of whom had any children of their own.

All of the pieces were coming together in this nutty puzzle. My father's grief wasn't a matter of money or cruelty; it was about his Honeypot legacy.

"How about you help Grandpa Clarence with his work?" I asked Chester, who leapt through mud piles toward my father.

"Dibs on the goose!" he shouted.

For the next few hours, I sat with Apple and my mother, watching my son, father, brothers, and Chuck load wooden planks onto the goose. Chester was making a great impression with everyone; he was more of a Clarence than I ever was. Seeing how gleefully he acted around my father was an unexpected joy.

It didn't take long for Braxton to return with several of his raccoon thugs. "So, have you given my proposal some thought? First, we can handle the payment of the contracts, then discuss our green-hut buildout."

"Yes, I have given it some thought," I said, cleaning my glasses. "Your strong-wing tactics didn't work before and they won't work now. I'm happy to review the contracts with my attorney. You remember Sue-Ann Jolie, right?"

"The famed Gray Arrow," he mumbled resentfully. "She still works with you?"

"Not only works with us, but she and my wife are practically sisters. On behalf of all the Honeypots, we're not paying a sliver of a shell until Sue-Ann reviews the contract. Unless you have a problem with—how did you put it? 'Laws that we abide by'?"

My father pelted Braxton away with his cane and sat down next to us. "Now, where was that brain an' fire when you were in charge of CC&C?"

"Grandfather, did you know my father, your son, discovered roasting with fire?" asked Apple as she stood up tall, arms folded. Wearing a blue dress that matched my mother's, she continued, "you should have more respect for your family!"

"Oh dear, that's very kind of you to say, Apple," I said, frantically moving her away from my father's cane. "Let's not talk to Grandpa Clarence in that tone, okay?"

"Flippin' filberts! Yer a ferocious little chipper, aren't ya?" my father shouted with a smile while poking Apple with his cane. "What else you got in that big ol' brain of yers?"

"Loads! Where do I begin?" She hopped around in circles. "Mr. McFudden, would you mind giving us some personal space? This is a private, family matter." Apple then shared her extensive knowledge of various languages, including her latest addition, the dialect of southeastern salamanders.

Afterwards, I sat with my father and listened to the old, crotchety chipmunk recount all the mistakes I had made at CC&C as a child. He had a mouthful of complaints that lasted a long while. By midafternoon, my father opened up to me about his inability to sleep after the loss of my brothers and sisters. My mother was his saving grace-berry; he would have become chipwrecked without her. Much like a filbert nut, my father had a tough shell on the outside, but a soft core on the inside.

He later actually admitted his fondness for my roasted hazelnuts.

We prepared to stay an extra night at the Serenity Falls shelter-dome before heading home. Our plan was to take my folks, Chuck, and the kids back to Elderwood at first dawn. Then, returning with Sue-Ann, Chuck and I would come straight back for the rest of my brothers.

As we prepared for bed by sanitizing our sleeping arrangements, I noticed my father sitting on a chair by the fire, waving for me to join him.

"Shouldn't you be sleeping, old-chipper?" I joked.

"You got anythin' to say to me, son?"

"Straight to the drama. Let's see, you were never that nice to me as a child. What do you want me to say?"

"Cause yer not a Clarence, you know," he said, coughing a little. "Yer different, an' I never liked anything different."

We sat next to each other for a while without saying a word, hypnotized by the fire and the crackling of the pine wood.

Thunder rumbled in the distance, snapping me out of a trance.

"Well, I'm off to bed," I said, noticing his dark eyes were tearing up. "What's with the tears? Did you burn yourself?"

"I'm sorry, Rockford. Fer any pain you felt as a puppy an'

in your life. Hope you can forgive me." He wiped a tear from his cheek and closed his eyes.

Before I could respond, he was snoring.

As a child, my father's pride left me a stray.

As an adult, his humility earned my love.

"I forgive you," I whispered.

I tried to imagine the years of pent-up anger he had carried, weighing him down like a wet log. Unable to sleep a wink that night, I wrote in my journal.

Holding on to anger and pain doesn't nourish one's happy self. My father's rage nibbled at his heart like termites, but tonight I witnessed an act of extraordinary love.

As I sit in this dome writing, it's not just the stinky beavers snoring next to us that nab my attention, it's the families huddled together during this difficult time. They have no tree-huts, and their limited food leaves them as hungry as they are hairy. Still, they are united under one roof because of their hopes and dreams for a greener future.

Most of my family is finally united after all these moons. It's up to me to keep our Honeypot legacy blossoming. This is just the start of my next voyage.

P.S.: Don't forget to sanitize your left hind paw. You stepped in something earlier and it's still sticky.

CHAPTER 26
A NEW PATH

WHOOOOOOSH!

My mother held me tighter than vines on a tree trunk as we flew from Serenity Falls to Elderwood on the back of a red-tailed hawk. There's truly no experience that can prepare you for the fast speeds of hawk-gliding above massive canyons and forest craters. I had to remind my father to keep his mouth closed or his cheeks would puff out like a parachute and knock him off!

After the three-hour flight, we arrived back in Elderwood to find Jewel, Sue-Ann, and the girls enjoying fresh lemon tea in the sun.

"She's beautiful!" my mother yelled loudly enough to pop my eardrum.

Before I knew it, my parents were squeezing Jewel, Lily, and Olive with love. I couldn't have imagined this moment to be any better.

"We did it, Rocky." Chuck put his arm around me. "Do we

really have to go back and get your brothers? They didn't seem to care."

"You're not the only one who thought of that. But in the spirit of family and new beginnings, we probably shouldn't leave them there," I said, sharing a laugh with Chuck.

"Yer wife is pretty. Who woulda thunk my boy Rockford would catch such a dame?" my father barked brashly.

I turned to Jewel. "You aren't gonna like this. Braxton has the whole town of Serenity Falls under a new contract, forcing them to work for lumber."

"Braxton McFudden is doing what?" Sue-Ann shouted. "There's no chance that contract holds two drops to a clover. I'm coming with you!"

"I understand, lovepot. Why don't you go now while it's still early?" Jewel asked.

"What's fer breakfast? I'm starvin'!" demanded my father.

"Right? Flying makes me hungry!" echoed Chuck.

"Come with me, Clarence." Jewel grabbed his arm. "We've prepared some of Rockford's favorite rosemary roasted nuts and fruits."

"Rockford made these?" he mumbled while sniffing the air.

"Just don't eat nightshade berries. Save those for Rocky!" Chuck joked.

"Too soon, precious," Sue-Ann whispered in his ear, "too soon."

After a scrumptious breakfast, it was time to return back to Serenity Falls and fulfill our promise. Apple and Chester begged to go back—they wouldn't take no for an answer.

"Round two, Daddy." Apple lay down the map of the forest with her crayons. "What's our plan this time around?"

"Our plan is as simple as a basil leaf." I continued, "Getting two hawks to pick up the group of Clarences won't be the biggest problem of the day. It's negotiating with Braxton's greedy ego and his contract that poses the larger threat. It's a good thing we have the Gray Arrow on our side. I think he may be afraid of you, Sue-Ann."

"Let's do this!" Sue-Ann chimed in. She held tight onto Chuck's arm. "Though I'm afraid of hawk-gliding."

"You can't spell safe without C-h-u-c-k," boasted Chuck, holding her close.

"Yes, you can!" said Apple sharply.

Chuck dipped Sue-Ann as if they were dancing. "Not in my world, beautiful." He gently kissed her on the cheek. Her nose wiggled with delight.

Apple and I rolled our eyes in unison.

"Here, drink this," Jewel passed me a cup of coconut water. "Finish the whole thing for energy. Apple, keep an eye on them."

We spotted the same black hawk with purple tail feathers. I could feel his cold stare from the tree-tops.

"AAAH! Abort! He is looking right at us!" I shouted.

"Once we extinguish the fire, he won't see a thing. Prepare to climb and mount!" Chuck yelled out. He held Sue-Ann's hand tight. "You'll be safe with me. On my mark!"

Apple climbed up my shoulder and held tight. "This one's perfect, Daddy. Depending on the weight balance of the Uncle Clarences, we can fit everyone on this hawk without the need of a second."

"Let's fly!" shouted Chester, now wearing an orange handkerchief across his face.

Moments later, my whiskers felt like pine needles flickering my cheeks. We were flying up through the canopy faster than ever! I'd ridden on the back of a hawk hundreds of times, but this particular specimen was by far the fastest. Even Chuck's adrenaline spiked as he clutched the feathers tight.

In a hair under thirty minutes, we descended toward Serenity Falls. Braxton was waiting for us along with his shady group of raccoons.

"I still can't believe Rockford T. Honeypot would travel on the back of that gigantic bird. Doesn't it have germs or bugs?" Braxton jeered as we dismounted the hawk. "All you need to do is sign the contract and write a check. Be a doll, make it out to McFudden Enterprises."

Chester plucked the contract from his paws. "This is the contract? It looks like gobbledygook to me!"

"Kiddo, you have it upside down. Let me take a look at it," said Sue-Ann in a soft, sweet voice.

"You remember Sue-Ann Jolie?" I smirked at Braxton.

"Ah, yes. The famed Gray Arrow! Welcome to McFudden Falls," he said, spreading his arms wide with a prideful arrogance.

"Give me two minutes to read this, please. No interruptions." She began to scan the document carefully.

Braxton stepped toward us. "This isn't a legal proceeding. You are liable for fees per each Honeypot signature in this contract. Not to mention our green-hut discussion."

"No interruptions!" Sue-Ann repeated.

Chuck moved in between Sue-Ann and Braxton with his chest puffed out.

"She's even prettier when she's smart. Right?" Chuck whispered my way.

"I can hear you," Sue-Ann said, blushing. "Mr. McFudden. I only have one question for you with respect to this so-called contract." She tossed the contract back to Chester, who sniffed the paper. "Are you aware this contract was signed only days after what some describe as the worst hurricane we've had in recent history?"

"Here we go." Braxton clenched his jaw while wiping a few drops of water from his shiny black suit. "Serenity Falls, along with many other towns, took on significant structural damage to tree-huts and establishments. McFudden Enterprises simply offered conventional building supplies at no cost to get Tropland back up and running."

"Was this contract signed only days after what some describe as the worst hurricane we've had in recent history?" Sue-Ann repeated.

"Of course! The storm was a week and a half ago! We provide lumber and materials in return for labor. Why do you all continue to pit me as the bad chipmunk here? I should be thanked!"

"It's very considerate of you to provide materials in times of need," she continued. "However, this contract requires each animal to work well beyond the actual cost of their tree-hut. That's downright shameful!"

"For howling out loud. This… isn't… a courtroom!" Braxton shouted. "We've got work to do here. Stop postponing this deal. Sign the contract. Write the check, Rockford."

"No." Sue-Ann stepped forward.

"Sorry, Braxton. The Gray Arrow has spoken," I said.

"Don't be sorry." Sue-Ann elbowed me in the belly. "In fact, this contract is worthless according to Tropland's federal laws and regulations. Clearly stated; any contractual obligation signed during an emotional flurry, in this case, days after a hurricane, will be deemed unfair and voided by any court of law."

"Bam!" Chester grinned.

The large raccoon thugs took a few steps closer to Chuck,

who puffed his chest wide.

"Need I remind you," Sue-Ann continued, "any attempt to stop us from leaving, including verbal threats or physical violence, will result in a criminal case that will surely put you and your bulky associates in jail."

"Rocky, I'm in love," Chuck whispered my way.

"Me too," Chester whispered back.

"Me three," Apple echoed.

Braxton flicked off another drop of water from his fancy suit. "I don't want any trouble, but look around." The raccoons surrounded us. "How many times do I have to say this? This… is not… a courtroom! You and I had a deal! You're outnumbered and outsmarted, so let's all relax for a moment. Sign the contract, Rockford. SIGN IT!"

"Yer the group outnumbered, fella," shouted one of my brothers, walking toward us from the dome.

"That bird got room for fifteen more?" another Clarence yelled.

"Daddy, there's only twelve," Apple whispered.

"Math is not their strong suit, sweetheart."

The group of steely-eyed Clarences stood beside us, chests puffed up, prepared to get their paws dirty if needed.

Braxton threw all the pages in a fit of anger. "Not worth the effort! Everyone else back to work! You owe me, Rockford! We're not finished."

"Was that a threat?" Sue-Ann asked. "If so, I'll go ahead and file the paperwork to restrain any and all conversations with members of Honeypot, Inc. In the future, you'll be required to obtain the expressed, written consent of their legal counsel. Do I make myself clear?"

"Yes," Braxton muttered with a nasty look.

"Excellent," she said, giving Chester a fist bump. "Oh, and

Braxton— if you ever want to have a conversation in a courtroom, be more prepared."

We left Serenity Falls on the same black hawk we arrived on. Just as Apple predicted, all of us fit on the hawk's back, holding on for dear life.

My brothers were quick to learn how to hawk-glide. They were captivated by the fast speeds and high altitudes. I glanced back toward them as we flew above the canopy.

It was only a matter of time before one of them tried something foolish.

As we flew over the great Yumea Canyon, the temperature dropped. In Yumea, the longest and deepest canyon of the forest, the terrain of the lush green tree-tops transformed to a rugged gorge with tints of red, orange, and yellow rocks.

The hawk's loud, screeching squawk echoed across the canyon, reminding us that we were merely tiny rodents riding on the back of a ferocious predator.

"How do I get it to stop?" Clarence yelled from behind us.

"You put your finger in his ear. It's real easy!" Chester shouted.

"Come on. Stop! Move! Quit!" shouted another one of my brothers.

I turned my head to see three brothers pushing each other, fighting for better seat placement.

"Quit hoggin' yer tail on all the soft space, Clarence!"

"I ain't hoggin'. I was sittin' here since we took off!"

"Will you guys stop fighting?" I shouted back.

"You ain't our daddy. Mind yer business!"

One of them tumbled backwards off the hawk's back.

"Clarence!" I yelled. "Chuck!! CODE RED!"

Clarence held on by a single purple tail feather, flapping around at high speed.

The hawk let out an even louder squawk as he tried shaking

us all off.

"Brace for impact!" yelled Chuck.

The hawk abruptly shifted his body to avoid crashing into the side of the canyon's vertical wall. All of us tumbled off, smashing against the hard rocks and landed onto a small, thin ledge.

"Everyone alright?" Chuck helped Sue-Ann and the children.

The hawk hovered close to us, its monstrous talons bared. We were pushed closer to the cliff edge with each pump of its wings.

"Daddy!" Apple shouted, holding on to my visibly broken leg.

This situation would have been difficult for any of us, but now I was a disadvantage to the group.

Another ear-splitting squawk echoed across the canyon.

"Chuck! Do something!" Sue-Ann shouted.

Lunging forward, Chuck yelled bizarre sounds, trying to scare the beast away.

Again, a fierce flap of his wings blew another giant gust of wind our way.

Chuck flew back, toward the edge.

"Somebody do somethin' or we're mud piles!" one of my brothers shouted.

Apple crawled closer to the hawk, squawking back as loud as the little chipmunk could.

"What are you doing?" Chester shrieked.

"I'm not certain, but his squawks sound similar to a harpy eagle," she said, then continued squawking.

Back and forth they screeched! All of a sudden, the great beast perched on the cliff edge beside us, tucking his wings away.

"I think he understands me, Daddy!"

"This is unbelievable," Sue-Ann whimpered in relief.

I was speechless. I couldn't believe my eyes and ears.

It didn't take much longer for Apple to start translating what the hawk was saying. Apparently, she explained, hawks can see great distances. He didn't trust Braxton and his gang of raccoons, so he waited for us back in Serenity Falls to make sure we were safe.

"His name is Ergo," she explained, "and he apologizes for the crash landing. The tail feather pluck took him by surprise."

Ergo wouldn't stop screeching with excitement at being understood. He even let Apple pet his yellow beak.

Apple translated, "Ergo likes helping us travel across the forest. He wants to know why you cause a fire every time you need a ride, Uncle Chuck?"

"Tell Ergo it's because we don't want to be his breakfast, lunch, or dinner," Chuck remarked.

The hawk let out a few screeches. Apple translated, "Ergo says the fire is irrational. He means us no harm and has no intention of eating us. He says none of the hawks in Tropland want to eat us. They prefer fruits and nuts."

I reached into my bag to toss the hawk a few roasted hazelnuts. We could see his black pupils get bigger with anticipation.

"Can you ask Mr. Ergo to give us a ride home? My leg really hurts," I said, holding on to Clarence as a crutch.

Another Clarence crawled over to Apple to sniff her. "You got magical powers?"

Ergo directed his large yellow beak toward Clarence, and with a burst of hot air, pushed him away from Apple.

"Would you look at that? Apple has a new friend," Sue-Ann chuckled.

CHAPTER 27
FACING FEAR

-Back to Green-Hut Market 39-

"Ladies and gents, we have officially reached over four million viewers," cheers Holly as she flies over the marketplace. "If you're in the area, come on down to witness history! If you just joined us or missed the beginning of hashtag Rockford Origin Story, the whole video will be available on my Whisker channel to watch later."

Theo, Randy, and Ann, along with some of Chuck's grandchildren, dance atop a table as the crowd claps with a beat.

Suddenly, another enormous hawk carrying three dozen chipmunks on its back descends toward the marketplace.

A few adults and a group of youngsters come running up to Rockford. Chuck embraces one of the older chipmunks, who wears an orange shirt and khaki trousers.

"Chester, my boy! You made it!" Chuck shouts.

"Uncle Chuck! Dad!" Chester embraces them both. His youthful face has aged slightly with time. He introduces his wife and entire family, including Alex, Theo's father.

"Pops!" Theo races up Alex's yellow sweater and onto his shoulder, jostling his father's square eyeglasses. "Best decision EVER to come here today! Did you know Great-granddad discovered roasting?" Theo backflips off Alex's shoulder toward his brothers and sisters. "Did you know Great-grandad knows an ancient style of fighting? He's gonna teach me later." He spins his yo-yo around his body, then retracts it back. "Did you see that one? I'm the Yo-Yo King!"

Theo starts fighting with his brothers, who try to steal the yo-yo from him.

"Your whole family is really sweet," says Ann in admiration, distracting Theo from his siblings. "Do you think Jewel and Apple will come?"

"Mr. Honeypot?" interrupts Ben. "What's up with the swamplands Chuck mentioned earlier? You didn't actually go to the gross swamplands, did you?"

"Who said swamplands?" Chuck looks out to the crowd. "Get this! We dive in deep on hawk-back, searching for the enemy. Rocky here nearly soiled himself four times over from the murky waters. I tell you, it was by far one of the creepiest parts of the forest I have ever seen."

"Chucky?" Sue-Ann elbows him in the chest. "Why don't you let Rockford tell the story?"

"Oh, right." He lifts Theo onto his shoulder. "Take it away, Rocky."

"Yeah. Take us away!" Theo echoed.

--

It took many years for Tropland to rebuild after what was

later named "The Great Storm." With major investments in infrastructure and utilities, Mulberry revolutionized the beaver power grids across the forest. Meanwhile, tree-huts from coast to coast were being rebuilt with reinforced wood courtesy of McFudden Enterprises. Despite his ill-mannered, greedy behavior, Braxton played a vital role in Tropland's initial recovery.

The animal kingdom was thriving with new corporate technology, yet still struggling to harvest a wide variety of tasty eats. Advancements in agriculture had slowly decayed over the years much like a forest floor. Times such as these called for new ideas, new creative thinking, new thought leaders!

"Rockford! Where's the paw soap? I know you got plenty!" yelled one of my brothers from the shower.

"It's in the shower, ya dummy!" yelled another one of my brothers. "Open your eyes!"

"I'm IN the shower! How do you expect me to open my eyes, genius?"

"Daddy, with all due respect, how are we all related?" asked Apple, reading a book while Olive and Lily drew pictures on my cast.

As much as I wanted to change the forest, I was limited to staying on our branch for seventy-four days while my leg healed. The entire Honeypot family, including Chuck, lived comfortably under one roof. I felt grateful to have my family together at last, even if it meant dealing with my dopey brothers.

Staying at home recovering reminded me of the nightshade berry incident years ago. Confined to rest, I had the good fortune of having Jewel by my side as always. We spent hours planning our next generation of green-huts; improving and fine-tuning the new designs that would combine the delicacy of harvesting fresh foods with the strength of Tropland's shelter-domes.

Except for the pain from breaking my leg in three places, this was one of the happiest times in my life. With each sunset I felt stronger. Visits from Doctor Boo, a young toucan prodigy in the medical field, aided my recovery. He said I had broken my leg so badly, it was a miracle I was able to hop, leap, bound, or climb at all!

Once healed, we could finally resume our adventures with Apple's new hawk companion, Ergo. He introduced us to his family, friends, and community. We travelled deep into foreign canyons, discovering the extraordinary way of life of colorful birds of prey previously not accepted in our society. Everyone assumed these birds, "Predators of the Sky," had no manners or morals. That couldn't be further from the truth! These giant birds took pride in watching over the natural order of the forest as guardians of peace and fortune. After all, they were the backbone of the AMF.

I sold some Mulberry stock, bought three acres not too far from our tree-hut, and hired a few crafty beavers to clear the land.

The mindful monks' green-huts perished in the storm at Eight Poem Garden.

Our green-huts were destroyed in the "Great Storm."

This time, we had new architectural plans designed to withstand nature's mighty temper tantrums.

The whole family helped with construction for the next eleven months, building carefully according to our newly developed designs. Enthusiastic to finish, I would stay up all night, reviewing every detail. I had pushed everyone to near exhaustion in pursuit of green-hut perfection.

Despite our best efforts, it was, as Chuck would say,

"possibly impossible." No amount of architectural intelligence helped us solve the greatest problem we faced: how to seal the green-hut, built with no angles and no corners. Jewel was afraid our dome shaped green-hut would once again be destroyed in a powerful storm.

One humid morning, after an early lemon pickup, we sat down as a family for breakfast near our green-hut construction zone.

"Can you pass the jam?" Chester asked.

"Which jam? Peach? Strawberry? Apricot?" Lily replied.

"Don't matter to me."

"Don't means 'do not.' 'Do not matter to me' is incorrect syntax. You're indecisive and have poor grammar," observed Apple.

One of the Clarences tossed jam to Chester.

"Thanks. Wasn't so hard, was it?" Chester replied.

"This kid's a hoot!" said my father, laughing while coughing.

"I love you, brother," Lily said. "I love everyone!"

"When are ya gonna fix this green-hut of yers?" my father grumbled, his terrible garlic breath carrying across the table. "If Billy Fence can build computers, why can't you build a hut?"

"It's not that simple, Father," I explained. "Animals are not stronger than nature. Computers are manufactured with components using tools and materials developed in recent years. A green-hut construction of this magnitude has never been built before."

"So? Ask that boy Braxton. He can help like he done built the domes."

"Oh, horseradish!" I yelled.

"Rockford, we don't use that word!" my mother lashed out.

"Forgive me, I'm a bit ruffled lately," I corrected myself. "A shelter-dome is stinky, sticky, and littered with mosquitos. Would you eat a tomato grown in that environment?"

"I would if it was in salsa," my father said, stuffing his face with peach jam.

"Oh! Do we have any salsa, Grandma?" requested Chester.

A few seconds passed without a word from the table, a rare moment with this rowdy group.

My mother was staring out toward the tree-tops, deep in thought.

"What's wrong, Emma?" asked Jewel, concerned.

"Oh nothing," she mumbled, returning her gaze to the family. "It's just… I don't quite fully understand the problem we're having with the green-hut."

"Imagine carving a hole inside a watermelon without any juice spilling out," I explained. "It's not the materials that are limiting us; we have the watermelon. We need to develop new techniques, new tools to carve such a hole."

"Horseradish, Dad! The juice will spill all over the place!" Chester shouted, throwing his arms in the air.

"Watch it, Chester!" snapped Jewel.

My mother scooched closer to me. "Rockford, do you recall in book two of Captain James T. when Chester escapes the woolly monkeys of Mountain Valley?"

"Of course."

"I don't. What happened?" Chuck asked, leaning closer to me.

"Captain James T. was investigating a mishap in Banana Springs," I elaborated. "Chester couldn't escape a vine squeezing the air from his lungs. As fate would have it, a fellowship of leafcutter ants climbed to the top of the tree, bit through the vine, and rescued Chester from his last farewell."

"That's right. The same ants that dropped a beehive on

Chester's tree-hut days before!" said my mother, waving her arms with excitement.

"Oof. That had to sting!" said Chuck.

"Oh yes, it could have been disastrous," I continued. "Fortunately, Captain James T. befriended the bees over rose tea and apologized on behalf of the ants. He later helped re-attach the hive to a safe place. Mother, what are you implying?"

"Learn to deal with the bees if you want to enjoy the honey," she said with a smirk. "We all know who may be able to help in this situation."

"I don't get it. Are we going to work with bees now?" Chuck demanded. "Honestly, I've got nothing against them as long as they don't sting."

"Oh pish, Chuck. Not bees!" I blurted.

"Termites," my mother said, nibbling on a peach.

"Not a chance in my nuggets yer gonna friend them termite vermin!" my father yelled, throwing his plate across the table.

"It's a bit extreme, Emma," Jewel agreed. "While I'm thoroughly impressed by your Captain James T. reference, the termites are notorious mobsters. Even if we can find them, they most likely won't even talk to us."

"Grandmother?" Apple said thoughtfully. "You're saying the termites can improve on the architecture by their unique means of eating habits? Chomping through wood? It's unconventional. It's not sanitary. But it is possible! Chester, they could help carve that hole in the watermelon."

"Ooooh," mused Chester.

"Captain James T. is a story, Mother!" I blurted. "These are termites, not fictional ants! Have you gone mad?"

Everyone looked at me like I was toucan-cuckoo. My paws felt sweaty. Too many times I had been plagued by sorrow, fear, and anger from those nasty insects. The termites had demolished our hut twice, stolen my unshelled diamond, and caused me nightmares for years!

Chuck placed his paw on my back. "Think about it, Rocky. What if—and a BIG what if—the termites can actually help shape the materials? It could change the forest. I'm pretty sure I remember how to get to the swamps."

"They're right," Jewel said, as if thinking aloud. "Termites are the most advanced woodcutters in Tropland. The method by which they eat wood could help us seal the green-hut to be as strong as the shelter-domes. Probably as strong as a sequoia tree! Emma, what makes you think they'd be willing to make a deal? They're thugs who live by their own set of rules."

"I don't have all the answers," said my mother, tossing my purple amethyst stone to me. "Sometimes you just need to look at a problem from a different angle."

Once again, my mother's gentle wisdom provided confidence and clarity.

Could termites possibly be the answer to our problem?

The mere thought of facing termites made me queasy with fear and disgust, yet I knew this might be our only hope. I pictured the vile swamplands as a grotesque, decayed, stink-filled river of unsanitary waters with poisonous animals who didn't share my fondness for pineapple-plum bath bubbles.

No amount of paw soap could do justice for this path ahead.

CHAPTER 28
A DEAL WITH FEAR

It took only a few days to prepare, both mentally and physically for our voyage to the bowels of the forest. As a sign of "paying it forward," Chester volunteered to stay home looking after his sisters. Jewel, Chuck, Sue-Ann, and Apple would accompany me to the dark swamplands in search of the sinister termite colony.

We decided not to bathe for a week before our journey in order to "smell the part," as Chuck assured us. Ergo picked us up early in the morning before sunrise. Picture this: flying high above the forest canopy as the shimmering orange sun rises in the distance. The sky glowed with hues of pink, orange, and yellow from the chilly ice crystals in the clouds, while the tips of the tallest trees poked out through the morning fog blanketing the forest.

It didn't take long for the fog to evaporate as we approached the dark wetlands. The trees, leaves, and vines were all shades of muddy green above the dirty swamp water.

The slow-moving water was by far the most dense, germ-contaminated part of the entire forest I'd ever seen. Swamp insects, disease-infested animals, and frogs poisonous to the touch were just a pawful of the reasons we were terrified to be there.

"Been a long while since we flew near these woods," Chuck said as we leapt from branch to branch above water. He smelled like rotten tomatoes. "If my memory serves me, the termite colony should be this way."

Far too many snakes, lizards, and insects gave us the stink-eye as we passed through their territory. Several times we had to balance on a decayed log and paddle across waters where bright green algae, bacteria, and fungus would out-stink a skunk. Combined with the unusual buzzing, rattling, and screeches splitting the air, we were suddenly living my worst nightmare.

"Should be just across the water by those blue glowing berries," Chuck declared, pointing toward a lengthy stretch of swamp.

"I certainly hope so," I said. "I'll need to get this jacket cleaned at least four times over."

"Thank goodness I didn't wear my Louis Gentoo jacket," Sue-Ann grimaced. "Do you see all those frogs?"

"Brown and yellow markings. Map tree frogs," Apple recited as we all paddled forward.

Eight small frogs stood on a log, wearing only black shorts, no shirts. Each held sticks with sharp points. Behind them was a forest of mangrove trees growing from the mucky water.

"No cross," one of them declared in a voice that was surprisingly deep and intimidating for such a small frog.

"Hi. We're looking for the termite colony. I believe it's right over there, attached to that tree. We'll only be a few minutes,"

Chuck said.

"No cross!" another map tree frog insisted in a similarly deep voice.

In the short distance, I could see several mud-like termite nests attached high up on the mangroves.

"We just want to talk," Chuck repeated with a louder tone.

"No cross!" a third frog demanded.

"We flew a long way to talk with the termites. We mean no harm," I spoke up.

"Flew? Rodent, you don't fly!" scoffed another standing on the edge of their log. "We got poison arrow frog venom on these sticks. Poison… arrow… frog… venom! Want a taste, rodent?"

"Be breezy, Poipu," the first map tree frog croaked.

"Be breezy? Do you hear this noise? They gonna get sticked!"

"We come in peace," I said, putting my paddle down and raising my paws in the air.

"Say that again! Say it again! I dare you!" he shouted. "How much peace you got on you?"

"Sorry about him," the first frog said to us. "Poipu! Be breezy."

"Easy breezy!" he yelled back.

The bickering frogs began wrestling with each other, losing focus, as we quietly paddled our way past them toward the termite nest.

"That was… unusual," Jewel whispered.

"Easy breezy?" Chuck questioned, holding back laughter.

Four large, hissing yellow snakes emerged from the bushes. Two more slimy black snakes surfaced from the water, surrounding our log.

The largest yellow snake's head came within a paw's length

of Chuck's face, his tongue flickering mere inches away. "Easssssy breezzzzy, you ssssay?" the snake hissed with a scary lisp.

As we were escorted to a tall, isolated tree, stinky snakes, frogs, and an incalculable number of buzzing insects crowded around us. We were forced to stand on the very edge of a tree branch, prisoners in a foreign land.

"What part of do not cross don't you follow?!" demanded a giant cane toad as he came climbing toward us. "Out here, you answer to Don Ribbit."

"I don't know this Don Ribbit, but we came here to speak with the termites," I objected politely. "I have an important business opportunity to discuss."

Shrieks of laughter surrounded us.

"Have you ever spoken to a termite?" the toad asked, moving in even closer.

"No."

"Precissssely," a snake hissed in our ears.

A voice from the branch above us spooked Jewel. She grabbed my arm.

"Pay no attention to these loudmouth creatures," said a tiny blue frog with neon yellow patterns across his body. "You wish to speak with the termite colony, but you neglect to understand that they do not speak. I am Don Ribbit. Please, tell me about this business opportunity of yours."

For such a small frog, his voice was surprisingly loud. I'll never forget the look in Don Ribbit's eyes as he stared down at us in his dark brown bowler hat, smoking a cigar.

I felt a tickle in my throat from the intimidating blue frog. "Hello. You see, I intend to build large green-huts, but need the help of termites to shape the wood to proper dimensions."

"Let me stop you for one moment." Don Ribbit puffed his

cigar. "You ask a favor of me without introducing yourself? How am I to trust a chipmunk with no name?"

Sue-Ann stepped forward. "Sue-Ann Jolie, attorney for Mr. Rockford T. Honeypot here. This is his wife, Jewel, their daughter Apple, and their good friend, Chuck Goldblum. Are we to assume you are the legal counsel for the termite colony?"

"Legal counsel? I like to think of myself more as a job creator, with the termites acting as my noble employees."

"Mr. Ribbit," I said timidly.

"Please, Mr. Ribbit was my father, may he rest in peace. Call me Don Ribbit."

"Don Ribbit," I continued, "We have plans that could revolutionize the food system across the entire forest. With the help of the termites, we believe we can pioneer a new type of marketplace."

He stood there smoking his cigar for a few moments. We could see the termites exiting their nests above us, spreading across the branches like a dark cloud coating the bark. I noticed my unshelled diamond lodged by the entrance to their nest.

I felt the overwhelming urge to toss a rock right through their hut!

"Tell me, Mr. Rockford—" Don Ribbit continued to puff his cigar. "—I want you to take a good look at the situation. Does it appear that I'm in a beneficial position with this proposal of yours?"

"This guy freaks me out," Chuck whispered in my ear.

"He's so small," Apple whispered in my other ear.

"I'll tell you what," Don Ribbit gloated, "why don't you tell me about your business proposal one more time?"

He looked toward the termites, waving his hands around like he was knitting a blanket.

Apple's eyes popped open wide. "Daddy, he's using sign

language," she said, elbowing me in the belly.

"Ouch. How do you know sign language?" I asked.

"Really? That's what you're asking me right now?"

"Good point. What's he saying?"

"I think… I think he's telling the termites to lick the branch that we're standing on."

"I'm waiting," Don Ribbit grunted, puffing his cigar.

"Breezy in the tree! What I miss, boss-frog?" shouted Poipu, leaping up from below.

"Excuse me? Who invited this frog?" Don Ribbit snapped in a huff.

"Boss-frog, I was told to wait. Figured I was done waiting. Right?"

The other frogs lowered their heads in shame.

"You're done waiting when I say you're done waiting." Don Ribbit snapped his fingers. A yellow snake struck at the frog, swallowing him whole.

"Oh dear!" I said, holding on to Jewel while covering Apple's eyes.

"Look at this cute chipmunk family. One would hate to have such a similar fate. As you were saying?" Don Ribbit nodded.

The termites were slowly making their way closer and closer.

"My client is offering a joint business venture with you." Sue-Ann stood tall despite her fear. "Under a newly formed construction company, we'll agree to set terms, providing you can sign on behalf of the termites. I'll draft the contract; all we need is a signature."

"That's a better offer. However, I politely decline." Don Ribbit waved his arms, signing to the termites once again.

Following his orders, the termites immediately began

chewing at our branch.

"Not lick. Chew! Oh, that makes more sense now," Apple thought aloud.

"Tell them to stop!" I shouted.

"Ooohh, right! Good thinking!" She waved her hands toward the termites in the same fashion as Don Ribbit.

Seconds later, the termites stopped chewing on our branch.

"What's this?" questioned Don Ribbit, tilting his head at Apple. "A chipmunk who can speak the unspoken language? With that, I am impressed. Alright Mr. Rockford, your daughter has earned you one more chance to present your business opportunity to me. Preferably in a more favorable manner this time."

I looked around in panic.

What did I get us involved with here?

"Daddy, let's just ask to go home," Apple whispered.

"This is not a negotiation anymore," Sue-Ann gulped heavily. "We may be in over our heads down here."

"I agree. Let's turn back while we can," Jewel implored, squeezing my arm. "I'm feeling very uncomfortable."

"That snake is freaking me out!" Chuck muttered. "Is it me, or does it look like one eye is green and the other is black?"

I couldn't concentrate with all the yammering. I needed to think.

Come on, Rockford, think!

"Daddy, the situation is unpredictable," worried Apple. "Our odds of leaving unharmed are rapidly declining!"

Aha!

I looked at my beautiful baby girl, her eyes wide open in trepidation. "The odds were never in our favor down here, were they?" I stepped toward Don Ribbit. "You want a presentation? How about a game? Are you familiar with

Mulberry?"

"That's where I recognize the name Honeypot," uttered Don Ribbit. "You hold part ownership of Mulberry. I myself am an investor, but own only a small percent."

"How would you like a chance to own a much larger percent?"

"Now, Mr. Rockford, you're proposing a deal I am very interested in." He hopped off his branch toward ours.

"Stand back! Don't touch him," I shouted to the group. "Poison arrow frogs are deadly to the touch."

"Rockford, as your attorney, I do not agree with whatever you're planning to do. We came here to negotiate, not gamble!" Sue-Ann exclaimed.

The termites surrounding our branch glared at us with their creepy, beady eyes.

I took another step closer to the poisonous little blue frog. "I offer you a challenge. If you win, I'll transfer ten percent ownership of Mulberry to your name—worth more than enough to buy all the cigars you could ever smoke. Which, if anyone hasn't told you by now, are very unhealthy for your lungs. If I win, we draw up a contract to form a new company. Let's call it… TTC: Tropland Termite Construction. We'll split ownership equally, and the termites start work next week."

Don Ribbit smoked the rest of his cigar, then flicked the ashes into the waters below. "TTC. That's a clever name. You're a clever chipmunk, Mr. Rockford, and it appears both options have a crunchy filling. However, when I win, I get half the stock you own in Mulberry."

"IF you win, it's a deal."

Don Ribbit laughed with rest of the swamp creatures. "Look at the whiskers on this kid! Alright, Mr. Rockford, what is this challenge?"

You know how to play rock, paper, scissors?" I asked.

"You've got to be kidding me!" Sue-Ann yelled. "Are you seriously wagering your entire fortune on a game of rock, paper, scissors?"

Chuck held her close. "Let him work his magic."

With a treacherous smile, Don Ribbit pointed a new cigar at me. "You. I really like you! I'd shake your paw, but it'll drop you in three flaps of a butterfly's wing. One game of rock, paper, scissors. Alright, you have my word."

The stinky crowd gathered closer to witness the event. I was already nervous, and the hisses and buzzing did not help the situation. Even the termites got surprisingly close to Don Ribbit. One touch, and they too would drop like raindrops from his poison.

"You know the rules," I said loudly enough for all witnesses to hear. "Rock beats scissors. Scissors beats paper. Paper beats rock. If it's a tie, we play again. On thump. Ready?"

I took a moment to kiss Jewel, figuring she'd be upset with me. On the contrary, her kiss was passionate!

"Now is not the time for romance," Apple groaned.

It became so quiet, I could hear the swamp burbling below.

I turned to Don Ribbit and nodded my head.

"Rock… paper… scissors… THUMP!"

The buzzing stopped as a loud, collective gasp from the crowd echoed all the way down the swamp.

Don Ribbit stood there with his small hand shaped like paper.

My paw was shaped like scissors.

"Yes!" Chuck jumped up high, almost knocking everyone off the branches.

Don Ribbit looked remarkably pleased. After signing to the termites, they retreated back up the tree into their nests.

"I haven't had a rush like that since a time I'd rather not discuss. I am a frog of my word. Draw up this contract and prepare for our arrangement. Say hello to TTC, my little friends. You've got moxie, Mr. Rockford. You know what that means?"

"It means brave," Apple said with a grin.

"And this one is going places. Listen, if you're in need of a job, I know a lot of animal-preneurs in this forest that could benefit from that big brain of yours."

"Thank you, but she works with us," I said, holding Apple close.

"What a day this turned out to be. What… a… day!" Don Ribbit leapt back up the branches.

We stayed another hour while Sue-Ann wrote the initial contract. Sure enough, he kept his word and signed it without hesitation.

-Back to Green-Hut Market 39-

Theo raises his hand well over his head while tapping the ground with his hind paw. "Great-granddad. Great-granddad!"

"Yes, Theo?" Rockford replies.

"How did you know what Don Ribbit was gonna do? What if he thumped scissors? You got lucky!"

Chuck lets out a big laugh. "I said the same thing on our way home!"

"I suppose every now and then we all need a pinch of luck," replies Rockford, adjusting his vest. "The odds weren't in our favor, but I had a hunch. I put two and two together. Paper comes from wood, termites eat wood. It was worth a shot Don Ribbit would thump paper."

"Are you pulling my tail?" Randy shrieks. "You bet your Mulberry stock on a hunch he was thinking of wood?"

"The most bizarre, unpredictable ploy I have ever seen in my entire career," Sue-Ann says as she gets up and gives Rockford a hug. "Once we started with TTC, the rest is Tropland history."

Holly flies down to film a close up of their hug. "There you have it, Tropland. All seven million viewers just witnessed this wild, off-the-hut story! Rockford, the comments are pouring in like a waterfall. Everyone wants to know what happened next!"

"Oh, dear." Rockford takes a deep breath, gazing up toward the sky. "Success."

CHAPTER 29
MR. HONEYPOT

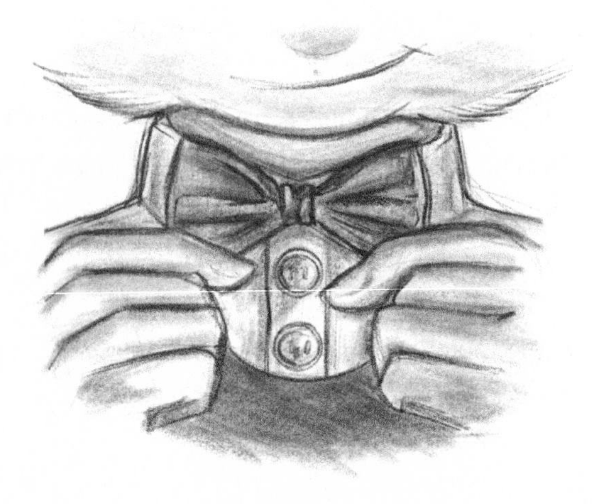

The forest looked infested as thousands of termites swarmed our construction zone the following week. We had to keep my father distracted inside our tree-hut due to his temper tantrums. He had been grief-stricken when termites destroyed my childhood hut. My father's temptation to go on a squishing spree was heightened. Ruffled by my own past memories, it was frightening to watch this colony of termites near our huts. At the same time, it was mesmerizing to watch them chew away at huge chunks of wood with precision, transforming it into screws strong enough to seal our green-hut.

With all the technology developed by Mulberry, the advancement of agriculture and construction was soon to follow. Who would have thought we would be the ones paving this path? Sue-Ann, our mighty attorney, filed all the necessary paperwork with the Tropland Business Bureau. Lo and behold, our brand-new company, Honeypot Inc., was formed!

After another year of building the foundation and

assembling the inner workings—remember, we needed to fine tune the controls of temperature, humidity, and light—Honeypot Inc. finally constructed what we called our own 'unshelled diamond.'

Deep in the forest, nestled between the trees, a dome-shaped green-hut of wood and glass seemed to sprout from the soil. Inside, a kaleidoscope of fresh fruits, vegetables, flowers, and nuts grew from end to end. A grand opening celebration was planned. Among the guests, we were happy to have Billy, Maude, and their kids join us that evening, along with Jewel's parents, Jack and Elizabeth. The vibrant colors and the sheer variety of produce blended delightfully with the colorful, welcoming animals gathered to celebrate the promise of bountiful good eats!

"To my sweet Captain Rockford T," my mother whistled to catch everyone's attention. She raised her cup of coconut water for a toast. "For every ache, a balm. For every woe, a cheer. For every storm, a calm. With each year, a new frontier!"

The crowd responded with a thundering round of applause.

"Speech! Speech!" Chuck and Billy shouted.

"I'm really not one for speeches," I replied, looking around for my fermented crabapple.

"Let's hear it, Mr. Honeypot!" A voice yelled from the crowd.

Mr. Honeypot? I must be getting old.

"Dad! Catch!" shouted Chester, tossing a crabapple my way.

I hurdled over the table and caught it with one paw.

"Thank you, Chester. As a child, I couldn't catch a balloon, but now… now I'm not just catching this apple; I'm catching up to my dreams."

I collected my thoughts, fixed my bowtie, and took three bites of the juicy fruit.

"Here's to who we've become… and who we've 'yet' to become. Cheers to both ears!"

We laughed, danced, and had a wonderful evening with plenty more crabapples. Aside from a drunk skunk who accidentally sprayed on a tree, I felt a true sense of peace. A real sense of accomplishment. A sense of the good fellowship amongst my family, friends, and soon-to-be friends.

No aches.

No pains.

No heartaches nor tummy troubles.

At last!

As the golden sun gently set through the canopy leaves, the full moon rose casting its glow upon our triumph.

"Nothing is impossible," Jewel gushed, holding my paw.

I kissed her cheek. "After all this time, we did it. Thank you for being my bushy-tailed lovepot. You are amazing."

She kissed my cheek. "I'm a reflection of your love."

THUD!

Chester jumped on my back, knocking us both over. "What are we, leftovers? We helped, too, ya know!"

My father walked over to us and poked me with his cane.

"Now what? Are we supposed to sit an' watch food grow?" grunted my father with his raspy voice.

"Do you mind?" said Apple, flicking his cane away.

"Time to take in the fresh, crisp air, and relax." I said, helping Jewel back up.

"Horseradish!" Chuck chimed in. "Here's a crazy thought: since Apple can speak hawk or eagle or any of the other million languages she speaks, we should start a forest-wide delivery service. We'll call it Chuck's Epic Hawk Gliding Company!"

SQUAWK!

"Apple, darling, not in my ear," I said, ears ringing. "If we do decide to build more green-huts, we'll need a constant supply of soil, seeds, and a whole lot more."

"My AMF squad will do anything to get back in the air!" said Chuck. "We would be delivering not only food, but packages… letters! Think of all the Nutty Nuts we could distribute!"

"Hmmm. With the speed of Ergo and his associates, we'd be much more effective than transport geese," Sue-Ann said, thinking of all the possibilities in her head.

Jewel wrapped her arms around me to keep warm. "I love it. This idea gives me goose bumps."

"No pun intended," added Apple.

"If we're gonna change the forest, let's keep this momentum going," said Jewel with that intense look. "What do you say, Captain?"

"Oh, dear. I think you know exactly what I'll say."

I looked around at all the eyes fixed on me, awaiting my response. Then, like a spring-loaded nut cracker, I bolted up to the roof of the green-hut and roared like the King of the Jungle! "To all the animal kingdom—may we never find a forest so extinct, waters so cold, bellies so empty that we can't fill them with love and joy!"

"Is that a yes?!" Apple cheered. "If so, I'd like to offer alternatives to the name!"

Apple spoke to Ergo, who then spoke to his family in Yumea Canyon. They loved the idea, but the name… not so much. Thus, Tropland Postal Service (TPS), was formed as a three-way partnership between Honeypot Inc., Chuck Goldblum, and Ergo Lontahuawkigo.

In order to get TPS up and running properly, I had to sell even more Mulberry stock, reinvesting it in Honeypot, Inc.

I believed in my actions more than ever! Having said that, I was scared cheekless! Flashbacks of bankrupting CC&C came flooding into my mind.

What if this plan fails and we lose everything?

What if another Great Storm obliterates our green-huts again?

What if the termites have a change of heart and destroy everything?

One very warm night after everyone was asleep, I stood in the flourishing green-hut practicing my minute limits. The full moon lit up the interior with a dream-like glow, casting shimmers and shadows throughout the plants, trees, and vegetation. From broccoli to pink peppercorn, it was a lovely sight for the eyes and a tease for the tummy. With each breath out, I released the negative "what-if's." With each breath in, I was calmed, especially since we had control of the temperature countering the fierce nighttime heat.

Jewel walked in with a cup of lemon sorbet, wearing pink pajamas.

"Can't sleep?" she asked.

"It feels like a dream, doesn't it? The way the moon kisses each plant with its light."

"Go on, spill the cashews. What's bothering you?" she persisted.

"Oh… I've been thinking a lot lately. Much of my success was based on luck, or 'divine timing,' as Sora would call it. I've conducted myself to appear as tough as bark, but sometimes I feel like a snowflake floating in the air, waiting for the wind to blow me away."

"Who's Sora?" she asked.

I felt my heart sink deep into my belly.

How had I never told Jewel about Sora?

I must have said something, hadn't I?

"I've… I've told you, right? During my time with the mindful monks, she was the one who looked after me and mentored me."

"I see. Nope, you left that part out of the story," she said, eating her sorbet in larger spoonfuls. "Why haven't you shared this with me?"

"She was a dove of peace who forever changed my life. Jewel, that was a different chapter in my story. You know you're my forever gem."

"Oh my golly! I'm not jealous." She leapt at me with a big, juicy kiss. "Haven't I ever told you that you worry too much?"

She jammed a spoonful of sorbet in my mouth, laughing with the most adorable flicker of her nose.

"When life gives you lemons," she said trying to contain her laughter, "have a big ol' scoop of lemon sorbet! Now, kiss me, Mr. Honeypot!"

CHAPTER 30
FAMILY REUNION

-Back to Green-Hut Market 39-

Several giant hawks hover above the canopy, the fierce flap of their wings create an opening in the branches for them to descend. Two dozen chipmunks of all ages disembark from their airborne companions. The younger ones run toward Rockford.

"Great-granddad!" They jump on him with a warm embrace.

"What am I? Leftovers?" Theo throws his yo-yo to the side. "No love for me?"

"Theo!" Randy shouts, grabbing the youngster and throwing him up over his head.

A confident female chipmunk wearing a light blue pin-striped suit and a vintage silver necklace taps Randy on the shoulder. "Randy, do you mind putting our superstar down? I know you two have become pals, but I'm not too sure Theo likes it."

"I can handle this primate!" Theo escapes Randy's embrace, then hugs her.

Ann taps the chipmunk on the arm. "Hello, Jewel. My name is Ann. You're totally awesome."

All the animals huddle closer, pushing Rosalina into the confident chipmunk.

"Forgive me," says Rosalina. "I didn't mean to bump into you, Mrs. Honeypot. It's a pleasure to meet you."

"That's alright, dear. Please, call me Apple. Rockford is my father."

"Forgive me, Apple," replies Rosalina with a caring smile. "Your father has been telling us the most wonderful story."

"I've heard! We've been streaming the whole thing on Whisker all afternoon. Would you please excuse me a moment?" Apple pats Ann's head, then walks over to Rockford, who is busy blowing his nose.

The two embrace affectionately for only a moment before the young chipmunks all scream "HAPPY BIRTHDAY!" and join in on the hug.

Holly flies down to get closer to the action. "Oh, snap, crackle, and fizz! That's right! Today is Purple Thursday and your birthday!"

"You bet your woodpeckin' pecker it is!" Chuck shouts to the camera. "Happy Birthday, Rocky T.!"

Sue-Ann elbows him in the chest.

"What?" Chuck protests. "Rocky goes and disappears for a few years, this is the welcome he deserves! Tropland, today is Rocky T. Honeypot's birthday! We had a big bash planned for the old-timer, but it looks like the party will be here tonight!"

The crowd cheers. A dozen hummingbirds fly down closer in order to drop flower petals from the air above.

"Aren't you tired?" Apple suggests. "Maybe we should end the story just for today. After all, we're supposed to be celebrating your birthday together as a family."

The crowd ripples with disappointment.

"Can we finish, pleeease?" Theo begs.

"Yeah! Pleeease?" Randy echoes, dangling upside down from a tree branch.

"I believe it's up to Rockford himself if he wants to continue. Don't you think?" says an elderly voice from behind the group.

Randy tries to flip off the branch, landing on his head near the elderly chipmunk. "Jewel?"

"Aren't you a delight? No, I'm Rockford's mother, Emma."

Everyone steps aside for Emma to reach Rockford with a warm, loving birthday hug.

"Captain Rockford T. Honeypot," she says, pinching his cheeks. "Look at all your wonderful new friends."

"Rockford rocks!" shouts a voice from the crowd, causing an even louder cheer from all the animals in the crowd. They all start chanting, "Rockford! Rockford! Rockford!"

"Can we hear the rest of the story?" Theo asks, jumping from Apple to Chuck to Rockford's shoulder. "Pleeeeeeasse?"

"Oh, I don't know." Rockford slumps a bit while wiping moss from his jacket, his posture not as grand as it was earlier in the day. "How about you show us a few yo-yo tricks? I'm sure our friends, family, and the millions of critters watching the livestream would enjoy it."

"Umm," postures Theo, sensing Rockford's sadness, "I don't know where I put it. Come on. Back to story time?"

"Story time?" Rockford straightens up. "You want to hear about when your parents were born?"

"Ew! Come on!" Theo grunts as Rockford giggles.

"Let's hear about Honeypot, Inc.!" a weasel in the crowd shouts.

Holly flies over to Rockford. "I don't want to drop a boulder on your shoulder, but your story is the single largest livestream in the history of Tropland, with over ten million viewers right now! Everyone from the ants of the forest floor to the librarians at Elderwood's bookstore wants to hear the rest of your journey."

Rockford kisses Theo on the top of his head. "I love you, Theo." He gazes out to his audience, all ears pointed toward him. "I have enjoyed this day and will forever plant this memory in my special garden. My adventure was full of ups and downs at every shrub. Before I continue, I want to thank you all. Rest assured that being here today has reminded me of who I once was, and the dreams that made me who I am today. Now, where were we?"

CHAPTER 31
THE REST IS HISTORY

With the first successful harvest of our green-hut completed, Apple appropriately named it Green-Hut Market 01. Soon afterwards, another powerful sto rm hit Tropland for six consecutive days. When the heavy rain turned to mist, and the sunlight started to peak through the canopy leaves, our mighty green-hut was still standing.

Word spread like fig trees that our marketplace could withstand Mother Nature's fury! Our Green-Hut 01 quickly became a favorite among both the locals and tourists for their year-round freshly grown food.

Billy took a shine to the green-hut and invested heavily. For a squirrel who could afford to buy every acorn in Tropland, most critters didn't know how well Billy understood the true pain of hunger. They only knew him as the billionaire of Mulberry, unaware of the dark time early in his career when he couldn't afford a pea or tomato for his family.

With Billy's sizable investment, we moved Honeypot, Inc.

to brand new office-huts within a business grove of kapok trees. The headquarters were built across four trees with our new logo painted on the front doors. Lily designed a purple heart as our logo, representative of my purple amethyst stone.

Over the next ten years, Honeypot Inc., along with TPS and TTC, created hundreds of new jobs, delivered thousands of assorted packages, and provided fresh, organic food for millions of shoppers. With the hard work of okapis clearing acres of debris, gibbon planners, construction beavers, hungry termites, muskrat deliveries, and countless other hard-working critters, we built thirty more Green-Hut Markets throughout Tropland!

Braxton spent most of his family's fortune building super-sized green-huts in an attempt to outshine and outperform ours. One heavy thunderstorm later, his green-huts were reduced to pieces. Demolished. Braxton, spiteful and vindictive, tried to sue us over nineteen times! Relentless as a wild pig in a buffet and a real thorn in my bottom, Braxton was challenged by Sue-Ann and our brilliant legal team. They countered every ridiculous legal action he took.

Chuck's success gave him the courage to propose to Sue-Ann while hawk-gliding over the magnificent Wabua Canyon waterfall. He built a custom twenty-bedroom tree-hut in preparation for the forty-three children soon to enter their lives.

As for the Honeypots? Apple was accepted into Elderwood University at a young age. While attending to her studies, she continued working closely with Jewel, Sue-Ann, and myself to run the business. Apple would later take over as President of Honeypot, Inc.!

Olive and Lily soon followed their sister's pawprints at Elderwood, then on to lead our creative division. They designed clothing lines, bags, packages, and everything in between!

Violet attended law school, following advice from the mighty Sue-Ann. She graduated top of her class, becoming the youngest attorney in our company's history.

Chester rallied my band of Clarence brothers, working closely with Chuck's daily business activities at TPS. As a team, we grew the company to be Tropland's premiere delivery service with their motto, 'Pay It Forward.'

My parents chose to preserve The Nutty Nut roasting business! Both my father and mother couldn't have been happier working with filberts once again. The Nutty Nut product line became the top-selling packaged item across all our Green-Hut Markets! Sue-Ann contacted Eve to create her own celebrity blends. She came by once a year with new recipes to make 'The Nutty Nut, Eve's Seasonal Mix.' Marketed with her face on each package, they would sell out faster than the sun sets. After all, she was now the top chef in Tropland!

Billy had planted a seed in my head many moons ago during the nightshade incident. All the excess charcoal created from roasting were repurposed as small tabs then sold as 'Honeypot Charcoal Pills.' They were an instant hit across Tropland, soothing tummies big and small.

As for Jewel and me, our quality time together became more scarce. I was either working late, travelling for meetings, or falling asleep exhausted on the couch. She was travelling across Tropland giving lectures on botany, the science behind our green-huts, or figuring out which foods to grow depending on the diet of the animals living nearby.

Over the years, we celebrated birthdays, anniversaries, weddings, and special events. We had grandchild after grandchild, and great-grandchild after great-grandchild.

Chester was our first child to get married. His graceful bride, Cece, entered our family with a wedding at the top of a bug-free sequoia tree. I had mild vertigo, but still nailed my speech. Apple later found love and married Doctor Mikey Lewis, a brilliant professor of mathematics at Elderwood.

It was our loving family that kept us grounded like the roots of a powerful tree. With every Green-Hut Market opening, the whole Honeypot family, including Chuck and Sue-Ann, got together for the ribbon cutting ceremony We wound purple vines around the front doors while a large crowd waited to shop the opening deals.

Two months after the grand opening of Green-Hut Market 30, Jewel was invited to give a lecture at Mint University in Northwest Tropland. I had slipped on a mushroom earlier that week, aggravating my old leg injury. Chuck was kind enough to escort Jewel in my absence.

I should have been there.

CHAPTER 32
BACK TO GREEN-HUT MARKET 39

"Oh dear. Where was I?" Rockford scratches his head. "I believe Jewel and Chuck left in the early morning. No, no. They left in the afternoon. Actually, they may have left in the evening?"

Rockford's expression is as empty as a hollowed-out tree trunk, as all the animals wait for what comes next.

"Great-granddad?" asks Theo, climbing up to his shoulder with a cup of coconut water. "Grandma wants you to have this. Are you alright?"

Rockford looks to his family, who all hold each other closely. "Thank you, Theo. Sometimes life takes you to places you never intended on visiting. Your great-grandmother went with Chuck to give the lecture."

"Rocky," Chuck interrupts. "It's alright. Why don't we stop here? Everyone is together for your birthday. We brought you a cake!"

"That's alright, Chuck," Rockford replies, petting Theo on

the head. "As I mentioned, it had been raining all week. Unfortunately, during Jewel's lecture, a sudden flash flood ripped down the mountain toward Mint University. I was told it was a sold-out crowd. Several thousand animals were in attendance, including Tropland's leading scientists, doctors, professors, chefs, students, and more. It was packed with the most passionate critters throughout the forest."

Rockford mumbles sadly, "I should have been there," then clears his throat.

"When the flood hit, there was no time to evacuate. The auditorium was built much like a shelter-dome with reinforced iron bark to withstand such a crisis. As Chuck later explained, the back door required a plankwood flood shutter for protections. For some unexplained reason, the shutter wasn't sealed before her lecture. Apparently, it's sealed every day of the year, but on that day, someone forgot."

"Rocky. Please. You don't have to do this," Chuck speaks up.

"You're right," says Rockford, his face turning pale. "Will you tell this part of the story?"

"Me?" gasps Chuck. "I don't... I don't know, Rocky."

"I'd like to hear it," says Rockford.

Chuck takes a deep breath. Every set of eyes in the crowd are glued on him, while Holly struggles to keep her camera from shaking.

"We were in the auditorium listening to Jewel's lecture when the sirens went off," Chuck explains. "A loud voice from an outdoor megaphone repeated, 'Flash Flood Warning. Plankwood flood shutter has been dropped. Do not panic.' I was sitting at the far end of the stage when just behind Jewel's shoulder, I noticed an older security squirrel fidgeting with the back door. Something didn't feel right. I tried to run toward them, but couldn't get through the packed crowd. It was chaotic! When I finally got to the gate, the security squirrel was in tears. 'Where's Jewel?!' I yelled to him, trying to open the locked door. That's when he told me Jewel managed to open the door and drop the flood shutters from the outside, securing the auditorium.

We felt the flood hit with tremendous force. Now sealed correctly, the auditorium was unharmed. She saved the lives of thousands of amphibians, reptiles, and mammals, including my own that day. I wish I would have been the one instead of her, Rocky. I really do! I'll never forgive myself, Rocky. She is a hero. You both saved my life more than you'll ever know. I'm sorry. I'm so sorry!"

Chuck and Rockford hug while tears roll down every cheek in the crowd.

Rockford takes off his glasses to clean them with a handkerchief. "Oh, my sweet Jewel, you beautiful lemon drop. You are missed with every breath I take."

The crowd is speechless. Even the wind whistling through the trees is silent.

"Thank you, Chuck." Rockford coughs a few times to maintain his composure. "After the incident, we decided not to publicly share what happened. We explained Jewel had a special project to attend to in the isolated mountains of East Tropland. Her heroic act remained a family secret… until today."

Randy raises his hand high while wiping away a tear with his other. "How long were you gone?"

"He just came back yesterday," Theo replies.

"That's true. It's been eight years now," says Rockford. "I couldn't take the weight of Jewel's absence in my life. I've been living by myself, isolated within the lush Yumea canyons."

Rockford walks over to his mother, Apple, Chester, and the rest of his family to hug and kiss them. "My family came to visit several times a year, but otherwise I remained alone, spending time writing in my journal and reading."

"Alright everyone, let's take a few moments for Rockford to collect himself with his family," Sue-Ann shouts loudly for all the crowd to hear. "We brought some cake, so I invite you all to stay if Rockford wishes to celebrate this evening."

Randy bounces over to Theo. "I'm sorry about your great-grandma."

"Thanks. This is new to me," Theo sniffles. "You know, I only met my great-granddad two times before today."

"Really?" Randy says, bouncing up on his tail.

"Yep. He came to our tree-hut yesterday morning. My parents planned a last-minute party for him tonight. Great-grandad wanted to get raw hazelnuts to roast. That's why we came today."

"He's a legend. Maybe you'll be a legend, too!" says Randy, attempting to bounce back on his tail and tripping over backwards instead.

Holly flies over, still filming on her phone. "Sorry, Randy. Tropland saw that happen."

Theo giggles, wiping a tear from his whiskers.

"Come on! I tripped on this box." Randy picks up a small gift-wrapped box and throws it at Theo.

It's wrapped in dark green leaves with a purple ribbon.

"Whatcha got there, fellas? Don't forget, the whole forest is watching." Holly tries to get close, but Randy uses his long tail to push her back.

"It's got a small note attached to the ribbon." Notices Theo as he inspects the gift, sniffing it and shaking it about.

To my Dearest Rockford,
Happy Birthday.

"Wait a tick," says Theo, "'My dearest Rockford?' Who wrote this?"

They look at each other.

"I dunno." Randy shrugs. "Apple?"

"Yes?" Apple spooks Randy from behind. Rockford is by her side.

"We found your present," says Randy. "Is it a new phone?"

"That's not from me," replies Apple.

"A secret admirer?" asks Theo, showing them the box.

"No, no. There's only so much love left in this old chipmunk's heart." Rockford kneels down to Theo.

"Enough love for me?" Theo gives Rockford a hug.

"You'll never run out of love from me," Rockford says, enjoying the embrace with a wholesome smile. "We may have had a secret admirer with us this entire afternoon. Where is that young lady, Ann? She has eyes for you, Theo."

"Oooooh!" Randy hollers.

"Pssh!" Theo gives the gift to Rockford, who inspects the packaging closely, then reads the note. "'My dearest Rockford.' Boys, what is this?" Rockford unties the purple ribbon, then removes each grape leaf one by one.

"Come on, already. Open!" orders Randy, swirling his tail around.

Holly does her best to get closer despite Randy's long tail.

Rockford looks around, then holds up the small box to his nose and sniffs it. His whiskers flicker.

Suddenly, Rockford's body stiffens, and his face turns pale.

"What is it?" Theo asks.

Rockford's eyes close; everyone watches him as his chest

starts heaving faster.

Then, his left knee buckles.

Randy catches him before he falls. "Are you okay?"

"Who?" Rockford clears his throat with difficulty. "Where did you get this?"

"It was right here!" Randy replies, pointing at the forest floor.

"Come to think of it, that sweet old chipmunk was sitting right here the whole time," says Theo. "What was her name again? Rosalina?"

"Could it be?" Rockford mumbles. "Where did she go?"

"I dunno." Randy shrugs.

"Father? What's happening?" Apple looks concerned.

"Rockford!" shouts Ann's father from amongst the crowd. "Saw her gallop near them shrub bushes some five minutes ago. Hey, Happy Birthday!"

"Thank you!" Rockford shouts, dropping the box while running toward the shrubs.

Theo picks up the box to inspect it closer.

"What is it?" Randy asks.

Theo opens the gift.

Red's Paw Soap

"Why would anyone buy Great-granddad old, expired soap for his birthday?" asks Theo. "What a terrible gift!"

CHAPTER 33
EVER AFTER

For an older chipmunk, Rockford can move! His plum purple jacket flaps in the wind as he hurdles over the tables toward the shrubs.

The entire crowd tries to keep up with the action. Holly is covering Rockford's every leap and bound from above.

"Rosalina!" he shouts.

A few hedgehogs point to their left, and he follows their direction.

"Rosalina!" he shouts again.

Perched on a branch, an elderly parrot points his wing to the right, urging Rockford to follow.

Holly crashes into the branches above, knocking over a cluster of acorns onto the parrot's head. He lets out an embarrassingly high-pitched squawk. A red feather falls from his wing and glides in front of Rockford just as he reaches the shrubs.

Hiding behind the shrubs, Rosalina is kneeling on her

knees, crying.

Rockford approaches her, out of breath, fixing his jacket and bow-tie.

"How?" he asks softly, kneeling down next to her. "How?"

Their eyes lock, filled with tears of joy.

He gives her a handkerchief. "After all these years. Why didn't you say something to me earlier?"

"You've lived such a life worth living." She sniffles. "I'm so happy I got to hear your story, and I'm so sorry for your loss."

"Thank you. All these years, I've wondered what happened to you. Sora, I didn't think I'd ever see you again."

A collective gasp is heard from all the animals surrounding them.

"I knew our paths would cross once again when the time was right," she says. Her tears slowing as she collects herself. "Does this mean you found my birthday gift?"

Rockford smiles like a young boy.

"Yes. Theo found it. I knew you took my soap!" He shares a laugh with her. "I have so many questions for you."

"I've thought about this moment for a long time," she says, wiping one last tear from her cheek. "For the record, we never stole your soap, Rockford." She giggles. "Mizu found the container after you had left."

"It's been a lifetime," says Rockford, taking a deep breath. "How did you know I came back home?"

"I didn't." She stares into Rockford's blue eyes.

"Why didn't you say something earlier today? For a brief moment, I thought it was you, but swore my mind was playing tricks on me."

"At first, when you didn't recognize me, I almost left," she says, shaking her head with a smirk. "As you started to tell your story, how could I leave?"

Several of the animals nearby sniffle, causing Rockford to finally notice the crowd surrounding them.

Theo approaches one step at a time until Rockford picks him up onto his shoulder.

"Theo. I'd like to officially introduce you to my old friend, Sora."

Theo's eyes sparkle like a twinkling star. "THE Sora? Nice to meet you… again, I guess."

"It's a pleasure to meet you, too… again." She laughs. "You have your great-grandfather's eyes."

"I do?" Theo leans in eye to eye with Rockford.

"You're too cute. I'm impressed with your yo-yo skills, Theo," says Sora, returning her peaceful gaze to Rockford. "It looks like you've got the whole valley waiting to celebrate. It's a long journey back home—I should leave soon."

"No. Please… stay." Rockford's eyes tear up again.

"Yeah, stay, Sora! I could teach you some yo-yo tricks," Theo exclaims, reaching around his pockets for his yo-yo. "I'll find it later. We have cake!" he shouts with excitement.

Rockford extends his paw to Sora. "You travelled all this way for a reason. Don't leave."

She looks up at him with wonder and love. "Each day a journey," she says, accepting his paw.

"A battle of blood or heart," he says, lifting her up.

"To live is to love," she finishes quietly as they both take a deep breath.

"And to love is to eat cake. Let's go already!" Theo bolts back to his siblings.

Moments later, everyone is gathered around, talking and celebrating, the tables arranged with a beautiful display of fruits, roasted nuts, and fermented apples for the adults. The sun having set, the full moon lights up the marketplace. Several lamps are placed throughout the area, with thousands of Tropland's fireflies giving the crowd a spectacular multi-colored light show.

Apple and Emma walk out with a cake in the shape of a giant hazelnut. They light a dozen pink and yellow candles as the crowd collectively sings Happy Birthday to Rockford. The look on his face is filled with joy and love. Theo, standing on his shoulder, is singing a touch too loudly, but he doesn't seem to mind. With the entire family by his side, including Sora, Rockford is happy.

"Speech!" Ben shouts from the crowd.

Everyone laughs.

"Speech? I just told you my entire life history," Rockford chuckles, the candles lighting up the whole area. "What more do you want? To read my journal?"

"Really?" Randy asks eagerly.

"Speak from your heart, Dad," Chester says, standing next to him and Sora.

Sora whispers something in Rockford's ear.

He smiles.

"Friends, family, dwellers of Tropland… wherever life takes you, stay humble and never give up on your dreams. Always stay grounded and true to who you are, no matter what quibbles happen in your lives." He takes his purple amethyst stone out from his pocket. "Theo, I want you to have this. Beauty is everywhere. Sometimes you just need to look from a different angle."

"Whoa. Thanks!" exclaims Theo, leaping off Rockford's shoulder toward a lamp. He holds up the stone as it reflects a beautiful purple glow onto Ann, who is busy twirling the yo-yo like a professional.

"This one is called the inside scoop," she says, spinning the yo-yo against the tree, then back around her body as she completes a double pirouette.

Randy shoves Theo toward Ann with his tail. He stands frozen next to her, both nervous and impressed. "Not bad," Theo mutters, cheeks blushing.

Rockford looks up toward Holly and her camera. "And to everyone watching at home, you never know what adventure is waiting for you on the other side of the shrubs. This is Captain Rockford T. Honeypot. Live long and blossom."

With a deep breath, he blows out the candles.

POOF!

A second later, the candles light back up.

Theo and his family laugh from behind.

Rockford tries to blow them out three more times, the flames returning after each attempt.

Holly flies up high above the crowd, pointing the camera at herself. "This is HollyBubbles3 live on Whiskers from Green-Hut Market 39, where we just witnessed the storytelling of Tropland's original superhero, Rockford T. Honeypot. Hashtag Rockford. Hashtag Origin Story. Goodnight, Tropland!"

Trying to stop giggling, Theo walks over to Rockford. "They're trick candles, Great-granddad," he says, chuckling, "Impossible to blow out. Give it up!"

"My dearest, Theo," says Rockford. "Haven't you been listening to the story? Nothing is impossible. I never give up."

He takes another deep breath and blows out the candles.

ABOUT THE AUTHOR

Los Angeles native Josh Gottsegen is an optimist, dreamer, creator, and passionate healthy living and wellness advocate. As the author of the children's book series *Joosh's Juice Bar*, which promotes healthy eating habits, Josh enjoys spending time with family and exploring new adventures with his beloved dog, Olive.

Want more updates on Rockford and friends?
www.rockfordthoneypot.com

Made in the USA
Las Vegas, NV
06 February 2021